CEO'S SPANISH FLING

JUSTINE LEWIS

ROMANCE

Recycling programs for this product may not exist in your area.

ISBN-13: 978-1-335-47083-6

CEO's Spanish Fling

For questions and comments about the quality of this book, please contact us at CustomerService@Harlequin.com.

Harlequin Enterprises ULC
22 Adelaide St. West, 41st Floor
Toronto, Ontario M5H 4E3, Canada
www.Harlequin.com

HarperCollins Publishers
Macken House, 39/40 Mayor Street Uppe
Dublin 1, D01 C9W8, Ireland
www.HarperCollins.com

Printed in U.S.A.

1 2 3 4 5 6 7 8 9 10 HDC 28 27 26 25

A dazzling new Harlequin Romance duet.

Cinderellas in Seville

Once upon a Spanish romance...

CEOs Mateo and Valentino's success has exceeded their wildest dreams. Over the past decade, they've taken the VR gaming world by storm to honor their late friend Pablo after his tragically young death. Romantic relationships, on the other hand, had to take a back seat...

Only now, thanks to the transformative presence of two enchanting women, it's all they can think about. And they're about to discover that love is much more complex than code. It's a game they must play to win!

In *CEO's Spanish Fling*
by Justine Lewis

Teo and Pablo's ex, Cara, never liked each other. But now she's in Seville, she needs his help and he's the only one she can turn to—sparking an attraction between them that sets his well-ordered life aflame!

In *Match Made in Seville*
by Michele Renae

Workaholic Val enlists the help of an elite matchmaking service to find a wife—only to find himself entranced by a woman who is his polar opposite: his perfectionist dating consultant, Amber. No algorithm in the world can predict the outcome of their unforeseen connection!

Both available now!

Dear Reader,

I love working on duets with other authors, especially with one as talented as Michele Renae, and being given a prompt like “CEOs and Cinderellas” is an absolute gift.

Cinderella is one of my favourite tropes (and not just because of the shoes and frocks!)

At its heart, it’s about overcoming obstacles to find happiness. You don’t need to be making your bed beside a fireplace to relate to the sense of injustice Cinderella feels. In all the best Cinderella stories, the relationship is equal and Cinderella also saves her prince (remember “She rescues him right back” in *Pretty Woman*?).

Cara and Teo both need one another as much as the other does. But with a complicated past full of heartache and betrayal, will they finally see it?

I hope you enjoy their story (and the frocks and shoes, of course).

Happy reading!

Justine xx

Justine Lewis writes uplifting, heartwarming contemporary romances. She lives in Australia with her hero husband, two teenagers and an outgoing puppy. When she isn't writing, she loves to walk her dog in the bush near her house, attempt to keep her garden alive and search for the perfect frock. She loves hearing from readers, and you can visit her at justinelewis.com.

Books by Justine Lewis

Harlequin Romance

If the Fairy Tale Fits...

Beauty and the Playboy Prince

Invitation from Bali

Breaking the Best Friend Rule
The Billionaire's Plus-One Deal

Princesses' Night Out

How to Win Back a Royal

Summer Escapes

Dating Game with Her Enemy

Fiji Escape with Her Boss
Back in the Greek Tycoon's World
Swipe Right for Mr. Perfect
Italian Tycoon to Remember

Visit the Author Profile page at Harlequin.com.

To my amazing, clever and beautiful sister Rebecca, who had her appendix out just as I was finishing this book. May your life be filled with handsome Spanish CEOs xx

CHAPTER ONE

SEVILLE HAD NOT changed at all in the ten years Cara had been gone. Not the smells, the scent of oranges and jasmine drifting on the breeze like a subtle perfume. The sounds were the same, the distinctively soft Andalusian accent and the guitar playing somewhere in the distance. But most of all, there was the sun. Hot, bright and ever present, warming her pale skin like a welcome fire. It was just as she remembered. The Moorish palaces, lush gardens, labyrinthine streets and shaded courtyards all remained impervious to centuries of invading empires and hordes of tourists. It was too much to hope that the past decade had changed anything about this city at all.

The last time she had been in Seville the events had been traumatic and life altering, but the group of people affected by them had been small. The city had not even been bruised, though Cara still suffered the aftershocks. A trace of the tragedy that had upended her life must be somewhere to be seen. She looked in vain for some trace of the man she had fallen in love with, but there was none.

It was just as well. If she was going to get through the next two weeks, then rule number one had to be Don't Think About Him. If she couldn't manage that, then rules two, three and four were mandatory: Don't speak his name. Don't go to his old neighbourhood. Don't seek out anyone who knew him.

If she could do all that—and, in a city of seven hundred thousand people, it seemed possible—she would be fine.

Only a job as lucrative as this one would have been incentive enough to make her return. She had resisted the contract at first, but her reluctance had been interpreted as driving a hard bargain and the client Richard Westwood had offered her twice her usual rate. When she refused, he'd doubled it again. Cara had been horrified until she realised that this money would be the last few thousand dollars she needed to engage the lawyers to take on her case against Liam.

She'd sent the email accepting the job with a shaking hand and now she was here.

Standing near the Puente de San Telmo, the bridge crossing the Guadalquivir River near the ancient Torre del Oro. The bright light and vibrant blue sky were such a contrast from the home she'd grown up in on Cape Cod, with its cool greys and soft whites. She shielded her eyes from the sun and rubbed the side of her waist. She had strained something a few days ago and was waiting for the pain to pass, but annoyingly it seemed to be getting worse. Over the river, a short stroll away was the university and her old neighbourhood around the heaving historic centre of Seville.

She would not be going there.

No. She was far better off staying on the other side of the river, in this part of the city. A district she had hardly visited with Pablo, but the pull across the river was strong. The memories were bubbling close to the surface. And try as she might, she was powerless to stop them.

Seville. And Pablo.

Every smell reminded her of him.

The charming, bright and artistic man she'd met while on exchange at the University of Seville. She had lived here for six months intense language study as part of her college degree.

Pablo was ostensibly studying but much of his time was spent creating characters and storylines for the computer games he and his friends dreamt of building. He was like no one else she'd ever met. Raised in a small town on Cape Cod, her trip to Seville was her first big adventure overseas. Pablo was compassionately curious. Charmingly quick. Devastatingly handsome. Heartbreakingly…

Well, in the end, simply heartbreaking.

Standing by the river she gave in to the feelings and let herself remember him. The magical night of their first meeting when they had talked all night about their lives and dreams. Being inseparable from that first meeting. The late nights and lazy mornings. She'd neglected her studies but had learnt a whole different type of Spanish not covered by the curriculum. Another language of passion and joy, longing and desire. The only language she saw herself wanting to speak ever again. Her concern for her studies faded as she realised that Pablo had changed the course of her life. The life she'd planned as a diplomatic interpreter was forgotten, her life would now be with Pablo. In Seville.

So when the unthinkable happened…

No. She had to stop. It had taken her years to pull herself back together and this short visit to Seville was not going to set her back.

She looked up at the monuments, at the bridges that had allowed armies to cross. Seville didn't care about her heartbreak, her memories or the tragedy that had befallen Pablo. The locals and tourists walking past her didn't care either. Each time she dodged someone she felt the pain in her side. An annoying pain that had been building over the past couple of days. Ebbing and flowing. Now it was accompanied by nausea and not letting up at all. Food poisoning.

Just what she needed. She could hardly cancel this job, not when she was being paid so much to do it. Not when she'd already told the lawyers to start preparing the case against her half-brother, Liam. All that she needed now was the last fraction of their retainer. But she didn't want to think about Liam and his betrayal because that caused a whole different type of pain, and right now the one in the side of her abdomen was all she could deal with. If she could just sit down for a moment. Rest. Get out of the heat.

There were still a few hours to wait before she could access the room in her hotel. She looked for a café nearby. There was a four-lane road buzzing with cars and bikes she needed to cross in order to get to the row of restaurants and cafés that promised a seat and a cold glass of something. Maybe even air conditioning.

It was early May, one of the loveliest times of year in Seville. The weather warm, but not oppressive. The jacaranda and jasmine were in full bloom, filling her lungs with their scent and decorating the colourful historical streets. It was no wonder this was the only city in the world she had ever contemplated settling in.

What had happened to Seville since she and Pablo had both left? What about his family? His friends? Cara had been in occasional contact with Pablo's mother, but that had fallen away over the years, as Cara sensed it just brought them both pain.

She should call Pablo's mother while she was

here, though the idea of doing that weighed heavily on her.

You'll be gone in two weeks. If you don't call her, she'll never know.

As Cara waited to cross the road, the pain in her side intensified. She needed to keep her mind off it and if that meant recalling things about Pablo, so be it.

She thought of Pablo's minuscule apartment, the one he shared with his funny friends. Chaotically brilliant Valentino. What had become of him? Was he doing something amazing, like they had always thought he might? What about Pablo's other friend? Stern, disapproving Mateo? Cara didn't actually care what had become of him. He'd never liked her much and the feeling had been mutual. They'd tolerated one another for Pablo's sake, but that was as far as it went. He was forever steering Pablo away from her and back to the projects they were all working on. Cara had never wanted to distract Pablo from his work or his studies, but the way Mateo carried on anyone would have thought Cara was trying to kidnap him and drag him off to the underworld. Teo had made his mind up about Cara without even bothering to get to know her. He'd barely even spoken to her in the five months she'd been with Pablo, with one significant exception.

As she crossed the road the pain took her breath away. She walked slowly to the other curb, finally grasping a light pole when she reached it. Maybe she should forget the café and find a doctor's surgery.

'Are you alright?' a voice asked. Cara couldn't even focus on the face that addressed her.

Then everything went black.

Teo put his phone down on his desk. His office was in the tallest building in Seville, the windows overlooked the river and his view went right out to the outskirts of the city and the horizon beyond. His desk was wide and neat. The view was blue and vast. The floor solid beneath his feet.

But for a moment it was as though he was back in his old student digs, its minuscule living room crammed with the computers they were using to build their first game.

Both calls were unexpected, though this call was as confusing as the first had been upsetting.

'This is the San Sebastian Hospital. We have Cara McCartney admitted as a patient. We're trying to reach Valentino Vasquez but he's unavailable and his assistant suggested we speak with you.'

Dread gathered heavy in his stomach.

'Is she alright?' He didn't recognise the sound of his own voice.

There was no love lost between him and Cara, but he didn't wish her pain.

'Her condition is serious and we're about to

operate. We are looking for someone to contact. A next of kin.'

'I don't know. I'm sorry.'

'Do you know Señora McCartney?'

The question was more difficult than it should have been. He settled on a reluctant 'Yes.'

It felt like a trick. Like he'd slipped through some portal and back in time ten years.

Except he wasn't in his old room near the university with the peeling paint and the faint smell of frying food from the café below. He was on the thirtieth floor of a new office building and all he could smell was the espresso on his desk and clean carpet. And he wasn't a struggling student, he was one of the joint CEOs of Verdadero, a billion-dollar company that designed and built virtual reality games.

'Appendicitis, but we believe it has ruptured and the infection has spread. She's been rushed into emergency surgery. Can I confirm that you will come?'

He took a few deep breaths but the dread was no less acute.

This isn't like that other call. This isn't like Pablo.

Pablo had not been involved.

Because Pablo was dead.

Teo's gut clenched further, not with fear but memory.

His oldest friend. The man to whom he owed

almost everything. His business, his reputation. His life.

Not in a literal sense, though it might as well have been.

When Teo had first arrived at high school he wasn't just short, spotty and uncoordinated—crimes that at the large sporty boys' school he attended would have been bad enough. Worse than that, Teo was an outcast. Untouchable. Unbefriendable. Even his teachers viewed him with suspicion.

Teo's life had changed the day his father had been arrested for defrauding hundreds of people out of millions of euros. A white-collar crime Teo hadn't fully understood as a fourteen-year-old, except that it meant that his family, his mother and three younger siblings, had to move immediately from their large house to a small apartment. And it meant that no one, not even his old friends, wanted to speak to him.

At a new school, with a newly jailed father, he had clung to the shadows. If he could just be invisible then he might just get through the seventh circle of hell that was his high school.

He watched life from the sidelines, until he noticed Pablo doing the same thing. But the difference between him and Pablo was that Pablo was an artistic genius. He saw the world like no other person Teo had known before or since. Pablo also stayed at the edges of their classes, not to hide, but to draw and sketch and write stories to go with his pictures. Pablo wasn't interested in maths or science but excelled at Spanish and history. And of course, art. In breaks Pablo kept himself busy with his pad and his pencils and didn't mind Teo silently sitting next to him, watching.

He didn't mind that Teo was shunned by everyone else. Pablo didn't care that Teo's father was undergoing a high-profile trial that was on the news every night. He didn't blink when Teo couldn't participate in after-school sport or hang out on weekends because he had to help at home with his brother and sisters. And when Teo's father was sentenced to thirty years in prison, Pablo had put his arm around Teo and told him that he must take after his mother. The only person in the world ever to do so.

Teo and Pablo hadn't seeked out Val, so much as become shackled to him when Valentino Vasquez was told to help them both with their maths work. But after helping them pass their maths exam, Val stuck around. He also didn't care about Teo's father, or Pablo's obsession with drawing and stories. Val had his own idiosyncrasies going on; perpetual tardiness, distractedness and most of all brilliance.

Teo didn't have Val's genius for numbers, nor did he have Pablo's artistic ability, but somehow the three of them worked as a unit. Val the maths whiz, Pablo the creative wonder. Teo just making sure that both of them got to class.

It wasn't until later, much, much later, that Teo realised what he brought to the threesome. Organisation. The other two were utterly brilliant but would get preoccupied when they were deep in a project. Teo didn't have the gift—or burden—of being outstanding at anything, but he was a hard worker. And he was methodical. And whereas neither Pablo nor Val could be depended upon to arrive somewhere on time—Teo could. He'd had to care for his brother and sisters while his mother worked, holding the family unit together throughout his father's trial and conviction. And everything that came later. Teo was good at getting things done. Teo was good at *being good*.

It was Teo who had suggested that Pablo's designs and stories could be a video game. Teo who had suggested Val try and develop the code for it. Not that either of them needed much encouragement, they were both ambitious, but they needed him to point them in the right direction. They needed him to stand up in front of the private equity investors to sell the concept. They needed him to make the deals. They needed him to rent the offices, employ the staff and pay the salaries.

Teo was a doer, rather than a creative mind. He thanked his luck every single day that Val and Pablo had put their faith and their creations into his hands.

He owed Val and Pablo an unrepayable debt.

Especially Pablo.

Pablo, who hadn't lived to see the success his designs and stories had become.

Pablo who… Teo's throat tightened and closed over.

Teo had spent his whole life making it up to Pablo, doing the best he could with Pablo's creations but this phone call brought everything back.

Cara McCartney was in Seville. That was surprising enough; he doubted she'd ever want to return after what had happened. He hadn't heard from her since the day of Pablo's funeral, a state of affairs that he suspected suited her as much as it did him.

Teo and Cara had never been friends. She had eyed him with the same suspicion many people did when they found out who his father was. And Teo viewed Cara with similar mistrust. Pablo had fallen for her deeply and eternally. Pablo would have followed Cara to the ends of the earth. Which was what worried Teo the most. He didn't want to begrudge his friend his happiness, but couldn't he have found that happiness with an equally lovely Andalusian woman, not an American with ambitions to travel the world?

As he hung up the phone, memories of that other phone call came flooding back. Things he hadn't allowed himself to remember in years. The nonsensical nature of what they told him still took his breath away.

'There's been an accident. A car mounted the pavement. Pablo didn't make it.'

Pablo had died.

Teo had gone to Cara's small apartment and found her dressed for an evening out, in a short black shirt and heels. She'd looked relieved when she'd first opened the door, but her smile had fallen when she'd realised it was Teo at the door and not the man she had been expecting.

Always the responsible one, Teo knew he had to be the one to tell her and suggested she sit on the nearby sofa. He'd tried to think of the right words but in the end, it hadn't taken more than a look from him. She'd turned from him and curled in upon herself. Even so, he still needed to tell her. She hadn't looked at him as he'd told her about the accident and Pablo's near instantaneous death.

'Cara, I want you to know how very sorry—'

'Spare us both your sympathies.'

'I'm truly sorry, if there's anything—'

'I don't need anything from you. You never liked me, so don't pretend to now. Just leave.'

'Cara, please,' he'd tried but her cry echoed across the room.

'I said get out. Go! Get away! I hate you! I never want to speak to you again!'

Teo had been torn, he wanted to stay to convince her to accept his help, but knew she'd never take anything from him. They were nothing to one another and now that Pablo was gone, they were even less than that.

So now, when a voice on the other end of the phone told him he had to come to the San Sebastian Hospital he wished, more than he'd ever wished, that neither he nor Pablo had ever met Cara McCartney.

CHAPTER TWO

CARA'S STOMACH STILL HURT, but it was a different kind of pain. It only sliced through her if she moved. So she didn't. She lay still and tried to make sense of what was happening around her. She was in a hospital. If not, she was in trouble, because there was a drip in her arm, her fingers rested on stiff sheets and a constant beeping was coming from somewhere nearby. She was being looked after, but where? And when?

The last few hours were a confusing blur. The pain had been intense and she'd fallen in and out of consciousness several times. Finally, the pain had ceased but she remembered nothing after that. Until now.

'Good morning, sleepy-head!' The bubbly nurse spoke in Spanish, with a strong Andalusian accent.

Because you're in Spain. Seville.

She'd known it was a bad idea to come back here and she was right.

'What happened?' Her mouth was completely

dry and tasted strange. It was still morning. The last thing she remembered was going to get some lunch. Waiting for her hotel room.

'Your appendix burst!' The nurse spoke as if she were announcing a party. 'It made quite a mess. You've had surgery and are now on a huge dose of antibiotics to clean it all up.'

Cara moved and felt the drip in her arm again.

'How are your pain levels?' the nurse asked.

'I'm not sure.' It was manageable if she didn't move, but when she did… 'Seven out of ten?'

The nurse went to the drip and pressed some buttons.

There was a lot to take in. Appendix? That would explain the pain she'd thought was just an upset stomach.

'Have I had surgery? I don't remember.'

'You were quite out of it, apparently. Which isn't surprising. The doctor said it's one of the worst cases she's seen in a long time.'

Cara didn't do things by halves when it came to Seville apparently. First Pablo's accident. Now this.

'The doctor will be around shortly on her rounds. In the meantime, we need to get you moving a little. Can I help you sit up?'

'I can manage,' Cara said, with more confidence than was warranted. As soon as she flexed her stomach muscles the pain gripped her and she cried out.

'Steady on. Let me help you.'

With the nurse's help Cara got into a sitting position. Just doing that was exhausting. Once she was upright, she could see the room properly. It was a private room, neat, clean. Reasonably quiet. She was glad about all of this yet had no idea what her health insurance was likely to cover. Or what she might be expected to pay. A different kind of pain clenched her gut this time.

'Try eating some ice to start with and then we'll try a little breakfast.'

'Breakfast? What day is it?'

'Wednesday.'

'So the next morning?'

'Yes. They operated yesterday afternoon and you've been asleep ever since. I don't blame you. You were quite sick. You still are.'

Cara popped a cube of ice into her mouth. It was refreshing on her parched lips and tongue. Everything tasted strange. The room smelt strange. No more jasmine. Just disinfectant.

'Dr Magdalena will be here soon, but in the meantime, you have a visitor.'

A visitor? Maybe Mr Westwood? But that made no sense. How would he know she was here? She had to let him know she might be late to the job. If she could even still do it. She had no idea how long it would take her to recover. Right now, her brain was a fog of pain and exhaustion and she wasn't even sure when she'd be able to stand up. Let alone when she'd be able to work.

'Who is it?'

The nurse grinned and wriggled an eyebrow. 'You can come in now, sir.'

Maybe it was the infection. The anaesthesia. Or simply the pain. But Cara was definitely hallucinating. Or maybe she was still asleep and dreaming, because there was no other reason Mateo Ortiz would be in her hospital room.

The nurse winked and left the room.

Definitely dreaming.

'Cara, how are you feeling?' He spoke matter-of-factly, as though they spoke every day. As though the last time they'd spoken, she hadn't told him to get out of her life and stay there.

'Sore.' Confused.

Deeply, deeply confused.

'What are you doing here?' she asked.

His face gave nothing away. That wasn't unusual for Mateo. Feelings weren't something he did. His facial expressions only covered the spectrum of annoyance to disapproval. This current look skewed more to annoyance.

It was a shame because when Teo smiled his entire face changed. Almost like he became a different person. She'd occasionally notice how he looked at other people, people he actually liked, and how different his face was to when he looked at her. Why wouldn't he ever just smile at her?

She'd never understood what his problem was with her.

He definitely didn't smile now. His mouth was tight and his forehead creased downwards in a frown as he said, 'The hospital called me. You gave them Val's name but he's on his way back from business meetings in Japan.'

She shook her head. She had no recollection of giving anyone Val's name, but then she'd been in agony. Who knew what she might have said. But that didn't explain why Teo was here. She hadn't seen him in over ten years. Not since the funeral. And she'd never expected to ever hear from him again.

'I don't understand.'

'Val and I work together. When they couldn't reach Val, they were put through to me.'

'Work together?'

'Verdadero. The business we started with…'

Teo didn't finish his sentence. But he didn't have to. Cara understood his missing words and understood why he didn't want to say them. Why he couldn't even bring himself to say Pablo's name.

'Yes, yes. I understand.' For once they agreed on something. He didn't want to say Pablo's name and she didn't want to hear it.

Pablo isn't here. Because Pablo is dead.

Something began to rise up inside her. At first, she thought it was tears, but at the last moment she realised it was something else. She covered her mouth and looked around for something to catch what was about to come out of it.

A plastic container materialised in front of her and she vomited. Liquid only.

She felt awful. Dizzy. Sore.

Great. She'd just vomited in front of Mateo Ortiz.

But as bad as she felt just now, it was nothing compared with how she'd felt the last time she'd spoken with Mateo.

Her current physical pain could not compare with the emotional anguish she'd felt when Teo had arrived at her door to tell her that Pablo was gone.

A woman in a white coat entered as Cara was wiping her mouth, saving her from having to look Teo in his dark and disapproving eyes.

'Oh dear, what's happening here?' the woman asked. She was in her thirties, with a telltale white coat. 'You're a bit unwell, anaesthetic can do that. I'm Dr Magdalena.'

'Cara McCartney,' she said.

'So I hear.' The doctor's gaze flicked to Teo. 'I'm glad we tracked someone down. You were all alone when you came in.'

'Mateo Ortiz. I'm an old friend.'

A different part of Cara hitched at the sound of his smooth, deep voice calling her a friend. It was a generous description of their relationship.

'Well, Cara McCartney, apart from just now, how are you feeling?'

'Nauseous, sore. A little confused.' That was just a soundbite of her symptoms. She was worried about her work, concerned what this hospital stay would mean for her client. And she was tired. Even though she'd done nothing but sleep for the last eighteen hours she could easily sleep another eighteen more. To top it all off, Teo was standing at the end of her bed looking at her with an expression even she, a person who spoke six languages, couldn't interpret.

'How much do you remember? You were quite unwell yesterday.'

'It's all a blur. I remember passing out, I think on the street, and some people helped me.'

'Yes, paramedics attended to you and gave you some pain relief.'

'I think that's the last thing I remember.'

'I'm not surprised. By the time you arrived here you could barely tell us your name. You had a ruptured appendix and we had to operate as a matter of urgency to stop peritonitis. We managed to remove the appendix and clear the infection using four incisions.'

Cara's gut clenched, causing more pain.

'At one point, we considered open abdominal surgery, but fortunately it didn't come to that and we were able to remove all the damage using just keyhole incisions. This will hopefully decrease your recovery time considerably.'

Good news. Bad news.

'What is my recovery time? I'm here for work. I'm meant to start the day after tomorrow.'

It already was Wednesday. No, she was due to meet Mr. Westwood first thing *tomorrow* morning.

'I'm afraid you're not going to be able to work for at least a week, and I would recommend allowing yourself considerably more than that. Two, if possible, until you return for your review.'

'Review?'

'Yes, we need to see you in two to three weeks to check the wound is healing and to make sure the infection is subsiding. You're not from Seville, are you?'

Cara shook her head.

'Where do you live?'

She shrugged. 'I move around for work.' Usually this was something she said with pride but for the first time in a long time her lifestyle was working against her.

She expected further questions, further judgement, but the doctor simply said, 'Then I recommend you stay in the vicinity for at least two weeks.'

'How long will I have to stay in hospital?'

'We'd usually let patients go home the day after surgery, but yours is a particularly serious case and we recommend you stay another night. You're staying with Mr. Ortiz?'

It was more a statement than a question to which they both said 'No' in unison.

'Well, make sure that wherever you go, you have someone to keep an eye on you.'

Would a hotel concierge count? Probably not.

'You have to rest for the next week or so, though I suspect you won't feel like doing very much. No heavy lifting. And no stairs.'

'I'll be fine,' she said.

Both Teo and the doctor narrowed their eyes at her, but neither said anything more.

'Dr Magdalena, do you know why this happened?'

'Appendicitis? We don't really know. It can run in families, though we don't know why. Has anyone in your family had it?'

Cara simply didn't know. Her mother had passed away when Cara was ten and her father seven years later. She didn't speak to her only living relative, her half-brother, Liam.

'Not that I know of.'

'It can be triggered by all sorts of things. It's reasonably common in people your age in fact. I'll check on you again but you can assume you'll be able to go home tomorrow, all being well.'

Dr Magdalena moved on to the next room, leaving Cara and Teo staring awkwardly at one another. The vomit she'd had minutes earlier far from a distant memory and still in the bowl in her lap. The sooner Teo left, the better.

'Thank you for coming, but you really didn't have to,' she said. *Take a hint and leave already!*

'They needed someone to sign your papers, agree to the surgery and agree to meet your out-of-pocket costs.'

'I have insurance. I can take care of whatever isn't covered.' She spoke with a confidence she most certainly did not have. Dr Magdalena had just told her she'd miss the next week of work, and very possibly the one after that. She'd lost her big pay cheque from Mr Westwood. She'd have to call her lawyers and tell them she wouldn't be commencing the action to recover her house anytime soon. She needed that money, she was running out of time.

'I'm sure you do. We can sort that out later. The hospital didn't have any details for you, no other contacts. Not even your passport.'

She nodded. She'd left most of her belongings locked in the hotel safe.

'Well, thank you again.'

If seeing Teo wasn't strange enough, this perfunctory conversation was at least on-brand for the two of them. They had never been close. Despite Pablo wishing otherwise.

Teo and I don't need to be best buddies, she'd said to Pablo. They had been polite, civil, but that was only ever as far as it went. They didn't get one another, but they didn't have to. Pablo was the only thing they'd ever had in common and now that Pablo was gone…

Teo was still not budging other than shifting his weight from foot to foot. Couldn't he get the hint and leave? A memory from last time came back to her. She'd yelled at him. She'd somehow forgotten that entirely. A completely understandable reaction to the grief she'd been suffering, but the memory still filled her with shame.

'Just let me know what I need to sign. My details are all in my phone,' she said and then gasped.

Her phone! *Please tell me I haven't lost my phone.*

Teo looked to the chair at the end of her bed and pointed to it with a nod. Her handbag was sitting on it.

'My bag. Thank goodness.' She moved towards it but fell back to her pillow with a wince.

'Let me,' he said.

Teo walked to the chair, and while his back faced her, she took the opportunity to study him. The gangly man she remembered had filled out, ever so slightly. But everything else was as she remembered, his muscles held his posture straight and proper. Guarded. Even from behind, his body language screamed, *Don't get too close.*

She couldn't help comparing him to Pablo, just as she still compared most men to Pablo. Teo was as tall as Pablo but that was where the similarities ended. Teo's face was closed, whereas Pablo's had been open. Teo's eyes were shuttered and dark but Pablo's were always looking for the light. For his next inspiration.

Pablo was open to the world's possibilities, Teo was always looking for the problems.

Just like now.

He handed her the phone and asked, 'Why didn't you see your doctor about your pain earlier?'

'I don't have a doctor.'

'Why don't you have a doctor?'

'I don't need one.'

'Clearly you do.' He looked around the hospital room with a glare.

Since leaving Seville a decade ago, Cara had been everywhere. She was an in-demand freelance interpreter. She spoke English, French, Spanish and Portuguese to the level required to interpret high-level business and diplomatic meetings. She could also get by conversationally in Cantonese and Japanese. Her German and Russian were rusty, but she knew enough to tell any presumptuous Russian exactly where he could stick his wandering hands.

The longest she'd stayed anywhere lately had been an entire month in London, working on a protracted merger involving two multinational companies. Once she'd been offered a one-year contract in Belgium at the EU headquarters. Cara had felt her skin crawl and her knees twitch. Staying in the one place? No. Never. She needed to be on the move. When you stayed too long in one place bad things always happened.

So what if she didn't have a regular doctor? Or a regular dentist. She was young. She looked after herself. Besides, moving around suited her. She didn't have anyone to come home to. She liked to live lightly, without deep connections. She'd already lost enough for several lifetimes.

'Can you just get off my case? What business is my health to you anyway?'

He gritted his jaw so tightly she expected to hear a crack.

'As I said, I was the only name the hospital had.'

'Yes, and thank you for coming. But I'm awake now, I can sign my own forms.'

He didn't answer. He didn't nod.

He didn't even budge.

'I can take it from here,' she said. All that was left to say was *Get out of my room.*

'Where are you based these days?' he asked.

Oh, that question again! What was everyone's obsession with her having an address?

'The world,' she said, and he rolled his eyes.

'Where do you *live*?'

'For the next week, here in Seville.'

'Okay, try this. Where does your mail get delivered to?'

She held up her phone.

'Your physical mail.'

'Not that I get any, but if I ever need to give a postal address it's in Ridgewood, New Jersey.'

'That wasn't so hard now, was it?' he said, and she thought she saw him try not to smile.

'And I've been there exactly two times in my life. My mail gets delivered to my friend Hannah's house and she lets me know if there's anything I need to know about.'

He shook his head.

'Just because my life's different to yours it doesn't make it wrong. There's more than one way to live.'

'I—' he began but if he wasn't going to leave her room he would listen to what she had to say.

'I'm not a fool, you know, I've been doing this for the past decade. It suits me fine. It's not as though I have a family.'

'None at all?' Everyone has a family, his tone implied.

'My mother passed away when I was ten, my father seven years later. Things you might have learnt about me if you'd ever bothered to speak to me.'

The skin around Teo's eyes tightened. His jaw, which had already been taut, was seconds away from shattering. It was kind of Teo to come to the hospital but he'd fulfilled whatever duty he felt he had and it was now time for him to leave.

Cara was so tired of being asked where she was from. As if it were important information. As though an address would define her. She had an amazing life, she'd travelled to almost every continent of the world, met so many amazing people and had got to glimpse into so many different cultures.

And the downsides of a nomadic life? Not many she was aware of. A mailing address wasn't the big deal some people tried to tell her it was. She never felt anxious moving around. Quite the contrary, she felt uneasy if she stayed in one place too long.

Home wasn't just an address, it was people. And Cara didn't have many people. She had friends, her best friend and college roommate, Hannah, was a case in point.

The one time she'd considered putting down roots had been ten years ago. In this very city. But the accident and Pablo's death had shown her what a bad idea settling down in one place was. It was better to keep moving. Besides, there was a whole wide world out there and Cara still had more of it to see.

A few years ago, after completing a job in Canberra, Australia, Cara had travelled to North Queensland where she'd gotten a small tattoo on the top of her foot. A turtle. She was that turtle, with her home literally on her back. She always used backpacks, rather than wheelie suitcases. Wheelie suitcases were a pain to drag over cobblestoned streets and getting up and down stairs. Most places in the world were not as accessible as some would think. Backpacks were the way to go.

So when Teo kept asking about her life, her hackles were well and truly raised. Teo, who had never bothered to learn anything about her in her life yet still felt it was his right to disapprove of her.

'Please leave.'

'I have to make sure you're okay.'

'Why?' *When you can barely disguise your hatred of me?*

'Because I signed the forms.'

Oh. Now she understood.

The nausea rose up in her again. It wasn't bad enough she'd have to tell the lawyers to stop work on her case, now Teo wanted his pound of flesh. 'You want money?'

'Of course not. Besides, we have an excellent public health system here in Spain.'

'Then what?'

Teo shifted again, back and forth on his long legs. He was tall. Or was it because she was sitting down, but he seemed to loom over her like a tall tree.

'I can't just leave you.'

'You can, it's easy, you turn and keep putting

one foot in front of the other until you're out the door.'

Teo shook his head.

'Why not?'

He let out a deep, loud sigh 'You wouldn't understand.'

'Because I'm an idiot? A child? What?'

'Because it's about loyalty.'

Ouch.

'What? Who do you owe a loyalty to? Because you certainly don't owe it to me.'

He glared at her.

No, not her.

But to Pablo.

He owed it to his dead friend, her dead lover, to make sure she was alright.

And because she had loved Pablo and because she'd never forget him, she fell back against her pillows.

'I understand loyalty,' she said.

'That's why you don't stay in one place long enough to have a doctor? Get your health checked out. Your teeth?'

Cara's face burnt. The nerve of this man! 'What's wrong with my teeth?'

He shook his head. 'Nothing. That's not what I meant.' Pink bloomed across his cheeks. *Good.*

'Then get off my case. You've come, you've seen me. You've satisfied yourself that I'm okay, now you can leave. Thank you for signing all the forms, email me my bill.'

'Fine,' he said through his teeth. 'Where are you staying? In case I need to contact you about anything else.'

She gave him the name of her hotel and hoped that would finally be it.

He nodded and then slid a card onto the table in front of her.

Mateo Ortiz
Verdadero
CEO

Blast.

Teo stepped outside Cara's hospital room and dragged deep breaths into his lungs. Being here brought it all back. The smell of the ward, the squeak of the linoleum under his shoes. Everything about this place transported him back a decade. To this very building.

To Pablo. It was so nonsensical, so strange. Hit by a driver who had suffered a medical episode, lost consciousness and control of his car before mounting the curb. Not premeditated, just a horrible, senseless accident. If he had been walking a second faster or a second slower Pablo would not have died.

Teo had been the one to formally identify Pablo so that his parents didn't have to. That memory unhelpfully resurfaced now so he did what he always had when it happened. He thought of the mark on the wall, just above the body, that he had focused on after glancing at his poor dead friend. The mark on the wall inert, inoffensive. Far better than what lay on the bed.

So seeing Cara, strangely unchanged after all this time, lying still, vulnerable, small in her hospital bed. Still looking at him as though she wanted to burn a hole right through him. It brought it all back.

At least she didn't scream at you this time.

He'd never done anything to upset her, he was sure of that, yet he'd never done anything warm to her either. There were reasons for that, maybe not noble ones, but reasons, nonetheless.

As hard as identifying Pablo's body had been, the visit to Cara's apartment had been worse. She'd looked at him and, somehow, she'd known; Teo arriving unannounced at her apartment must have signalled that something was very wrong. She'd glared at him with her big amber eyes, as though it was all his fault. And at that moment he'd almost believed it was.

I said, get out. Go. Go! Get away! I hate you! Can't you see I never want to speak to you again!

And there it was. What she really thought of him. He couldn't argue with her; he'd simply staggered from her apartment and steadied himself against the corridor wall. Just as he was doing now.

Pablo had been Teo's best and oldest friend. And Pablo had loved Cara in the same way he'd done with everything he'd cared about in his short life: completely, passionately, without abandon or reservation.

He'd signed the papers, seen Cara. Assured himself she was okay. Job done. Now to go back to the office. The deal they were working on was progressing. Verdadero, their VR gaming company had done many big deals over the years, each seemingly bigger than the last, but this one carried an additional emotional significance. A studio in California was interested in adapting their first game, the one Pablo had created, into a film. The deal was undoubtedly lucrative, would bring them more exposure than they had ever had in the past, but more than any of those things, it would also honour Pablo.

Pablo would've loved this.

The thought had sustained Teo over the past few weeks, ever since they'd first been approached by the producers, Jerry and Doug. Verdadero had received interest from film producers in the past but negotiations had never reached this stage. Val had flown in from Japan this morning and they needed to update one another on all the recent developments. Teo had to look over the specifications for their newest game. Attend a budget meeting. He had things to do.

Yet, three hours later he was back in Cara's

hospital room carrying the backpack he'd collected from her hotel. It hadn't been a simple thing to get it, but after he'd paid the bill for the rest of her stay as well as an additional and generous amount to ensure they kept her room vacant should she wish to return to it before the end of her booking they were more than happy to let him take her belongings.

Cara, however, was less than happy to see them.

'What?' was all she had to say but the anger in her eyes was sadly familiar.

'I thought you might need something.'

That took the wind out of her sails, the anger from her words.

'I was managing,' she muttered.

'I have no doubt you were, but I thought you might appreciate a change of clothes, your own toiletries.'

'They just let you take it?'

'I left them all my details, they know where to find me if I did something I shouldn't have.'

She took some deep breaths but needed to calm herself.

'Thank you,' she said finally.

'It's not a problem. Is this everything you have? Not another suitcase?'

'No, that would defeat the purpose. This is everything I own.'

'Wait, this is everything you have in the world?'

'Essentially.' She shrugged.

'Essentially? This is all your clothes. All your *things*?'

His sister took this much stuff for an overnight stay. Her beauty products alone would fill half of it.

'I keep a few things in my friend's attic. Some winter coats, that sort of thing. But yes, this is everything I have. And all I need.'

His face must have said it all. Wow. He thought he was a light traveller, and yet…

'I'm an interpreter. I need to blend into the background, I'm not supposed to stand out. Black suits are my work uniform. Those, and a couple of casual outfits is all I need. I sometimes buy new clothes for the change of season and donate the things I don't need.'

He recoiled.

'Oh, come on. I expect this kind of response from women, but I rarely get it from men.'

'What response is that?'

'Shock. You're slightly horrified, aren't you? Rest assured I wash and dry clean everything regularly. My backpack is the size of a standard suitcase. It's remarkable what you can fit inside it.'

'What about books? Mementos?' he challenged.

'Books are easy. As soon as I finish reading something I donate it to the next little library I see in a street. Or a hotel. There's no shortage of places to leave behind books.'

'And mementos. Trinkets?' Teo was intrigued, disbelieving and also slightly concerned, for reasons he couldn't even name. He too liked to travel light, but he had a place to call home.

She laughed. 'I'm not particularly sentimental. Life's much easier that way. Besides, I think most people have too much stuff, especially people in Western countries.'

He nodded, not entirely convinced but not prepared to argue the point any longer. A bigger argument lay ahead and Teo had learnt early in life to choose his battles.

'Well, thank you very much again. I appreciate it.'

Teo shifted from foot to foot, but didn't make a move to leave. He had to be careful how he approached this. How he approached her.

She hated him.

'How are you feeling?' he asked.

'Slightly better than I was a few hours ago. Still tired and sore.'

He nodded.

'Thanks again.' She rolled one hand in a forward motion to indicate he should say what he'd come to say or leave.

'I've come to ask if you will come to my place to convalesce.'

'Oh.' Her face fell. Not the reaction he was hoping for but better than the one he expected.

'Thank you for the offer, but I'll be okay at my hotel.'

'We both know that being on your own in a hotel was not what Dr Magdalena had in mind when she said you need someone to watch you.'

'How much trouble can I get up to in a hotel room?'

'That's not the point. The doctor said you should have someone to keep an eye on you. Not that I'll be watching you 24-7. But I have a housekeeper. She can check on you. There will be someone to call if you need anything.'

She narrowed her eyes, didn't dismiss the idea right away. Mostly, he was glad she didn't yell at him to leave.

'I'm not going to force you to do anything. But I understand you don't know anyone else in Seville. I know it isn't ideal for you to stay at the hotel you have booked and that you would be safer and more comfortable staying with me.'

She looked at her backpack and him, though her gaze didn't cross his face, but rather rested on some unspecified point in the middle of his chest. He resisted the urge to put his hand on his heart, which was suddenly beating faster than it should be.

'I know you haven't always warmed to me,' he said.

She scoffed. 'The feeling's mutual, you don't need to pretend otherwise.'

He didn't hate Cara, not in the way she seemed to hate him. But she was right, he'd always been uneasy around her, though he didn't want to dwell too long on the reasons why. It took Teo a long time to trust anyone. With Cara it might have been more than that. Something he didn't want to analyse further. The way his skin felt warmer when she was around. The way his body seemed to notice her presence even before his eyes.

'I don't want to impose,' she said.

'You wouldn't be. We wouldn't even need to see one another. Alba is happy to do anything you need. In fact, she'll be very annoyed with me if I don't get you to agree to stay.'

The corners of her pretty eyes twitched. She was thinking about it.

'My house has two storeys, there is a guest bedroom on the ground floor, with its own bathroom. My rooms are upstairs, you won't need to climb the stairs, or even see me.'

He couldn't have offered her a more ideal proposal, yet Cara shook her head.

Maybe it was time to bring out the one thing he didn't want to mention. He didn't want to do that. But if she left him no choice…

'Rightly, or perhaps wrongly, misplaced or otherwise, I feel a sense of loyalty and obligation towards you.'

Hopefully those words would be enough. He really didn't want to spell out why he felt these obligations to her. And nor did she.

He simply said, 'You know what he'd want you to do.'

Cara looked down at her lap. Her long, slender fingers played with her bedsheet absentmindedly.

'I'll pay you back,' she said finally.

'There's absolutely no need.'

He had no idea how much a freelance interpreter earned. He suspected she was good at her job, the Spanish she was speaking while ill in the hospital was pitch-perfect. If she could speak a language that was not her first under those circumstances, then she was probably an excellent interpreter. Though that didn't mean she had total financial security.

Fancy not having a fixed address! Flitting from place to place all over the world!

It sounded romantic to be sure but the reality was likely anything but. When did she relax? How could she when she wasn't around anything familiar? But most importantly, where were her friends? Her support network? Her *family*?

He remembered with a pang that Cara's parents had both died before she'd last been in Seville. He should have been more sensitive to the fact, particularly as he knew what it was to lose a parent himself. But what about other family? Teo's own mother still lived on the outskirts of

Seville. He knew she and his siblings were close by if he needed them. His mother was an active and healthy sixty-year-old and his family were all there for one another, his mother, brother and his sisters. He couldn't imagine not having them in his life.

No doubt Cara had friends all over the world, but it wasn't the same as having someone close by when you were in trouble. Or sick.

As she was now.

What if this had happened somewhere else? Somewhere she didn't know anyone. Somewhere he wasn't there to help her?

He shivered at the thought.

'Just a night or two,' she said.

'Two weeks,' he said. 'Until your check-up.'

'One week,' she countered.

He wasn't going to stop her leaving his house but hoped she'd feel comfortable enough to stay as long as she needed. He nodded.

'I'll let Alba know we're expecting you tomorrow.'

She bit her lip and nodded as well.

'Thank you, Mateo. Truly. I'm sure it won't be for long.'

'Yes, I'm sure too,' he said, silently vowing that she would stay until she was one hundred percent recovered.

Pablo would never forgive him if he didn't do this. Even though he was gone, Pablo still played a significant role in Teo's life. He'd come up with the idea for their first game, his drawings and stories had allowed the three of them to begin their business. Teo lived with Pablo's creations every day of his life. To say nothing of his legacy and the charity they had established in Pablo's memory. The Pablo Pascal Foundation funded various programs and projects to promote education, particularly for children who had suffered disadvantages. Children from low economic areas, children displaced by war or famine, and children with learning difficulties. Its portfolio was varied and they funded initiatives across the globe.

Cara would stay with him for as long as she needed to. Teo would just have to handle the unusual fluttering in his heart, and surely she could put aside her dislike of him for a week or two. They both owed it to Pablo and his memory.

I hate you!

Her words had shocked him. He knew he'd never been friendly with her, but *hate*? What had he done to her? Maybe it was the emotion of the moment, she was grieving too. But her remark had hurt, even the memory of it still stung now, years later.

Having Cara stay would be awkward, but it would only be for a short time. Then she could take her backpack and go wherever she wanted to flit to next.

He'd be polite, welcoming. They didn't have to

become best friends. She didn't like him, but she was wrong about him not liking her. Cara was smart, intriguing. Sassy. Good company. Very pretty.

More than pretty. Stunningly beautiful. Pablo always had had a good eye. But that was beside the point.

Cara was and always would be Pablo's girlfriend so whatever Teo thought about Cara was beside the point.

CHAPTER THREE

CARA LOOKED FROM her passenger seat to Teo, who was driving his small sports car through the oldest streets of Seville.

Earlier that morning the hospital had discharged her with antibiotics, painkillers and a promise to return for a review in two weeks' time. Cara had also called her hotel to cancel her reservation only to be told her bill had already been fully paid. It could only have been Teo.

But why? Letting her stay with him was already above and beyond, but to pay her account as well? She was undecided about whether she would say anything and this also rattled her. Usually, she spoke her mind without thinking twice, but something about this situation with Teo made her hesitate.

She shifted uncomfortably in her seat. Partly due to the pain in her abdomen, but mostly because of the uneasiness in her chest. She really was beholden to him, now that he'd taken it upon himself to pay her hotel bill. All out of some misplaced loyalty towards her because of Pablo.

Loyalty. And obligation.

That's what he'd said.

And it hit her. He missed Pablo. It was different to the way Cara missed Pablo, but he'd loved Pablo all the same. Pablo had been Teo's best friend, business partner. Like a brother to him. And Teo still hurt.

You should cut him some slack.

Or should she? Teo had never liked her, never bothered to get to know her. He'd barely spoken to her.

Yes. She remembered now. The feeling of confusion. Wondering why he didn't like her. What she'd done to earn his contempt.

Teo's dark hair was combed back smoothly from his face. *Never a hair out of place.* Literally. That was Teo. He'd always been like this. Unlike Pablo, whose hair had been long, wild, unkempt. Pablo who only ever wore T-shirts because the buttons of a shirt were too much hassle. Pablo who often forgot to wash his clothes and resorted to buying new underwear, a luxury he could hardly afford.

Not only did Teo almost exclusively wear button-up shirts, today he had paired his with a jacket. It was loose, on the casual side of business, but it was spring in Seville and he was only collecting her from the hospital.

Loyalty or not, she wished he hadn't asked her to stay. Paying for her hotel should have been enough to cover any loyalty he might have felt. If this car trip was anything to go by, her stay was going to be as painful as her stomach.

She couldn't give him the satisfaction of telling him she had little choice. She'd had to cancel the job with Westwood and on top of losing all that money it was also possible she wouldn't make it to Paris for the work she had scheduled the week after next. That was four weeks of missed work, missed savings, and missed opportunity to begin the case she needed to bring against her half-brother to recover her parents' house. *Her* house.

Liam. Her older, estranged half-brother who had managed to take most of her father's estate when he passed away. A confluence of a badly drafted will, an unscrupulous brother, and loopholes to do with her age and him being the executor and her guardian meant that Liam had managed to take most of the property himself, including her parents' house. Cara had been given some money that Liam held in trust until her twenty-fifth birthday. But by the time she turned twenty-five, Liam had managed to spend most of that money, claiming expenses as her guardian to take care of her, which he hadn't at all. Cara had worked her way through college and by her twenty-fifth birthday there wasn't even enough money left in the trust for her to instruct lawyers to challenge the situation. Which had probably been Liam's intention all along.

Liam and his wife lived without a mortgage and carefree in her parents' house. Her lawyers were helpful but given the low prospects of succeeding in her case, they needed money upfront to start the proceedings.

And now? Now the chances of getting that money looked increasingly small.

Teo pulled up on a cobbled street in a square in the old district of Santa Cruz. He opened her car door for her but when Cara lifted her right foot out, she winced. Twisting her torso was particularly painful.

'Careful.' Teo bent down to her level and his voice was soft. 'Take it easy. There's no rush.' He offered her his hand.

Climbing out of the low seat of a sports car was not easy for someone two days' post-surgery so she gave him her hand, completely unprepared for the sensation of warmth that slipped around her when she did. Comforting, strengthening. Soothing. All at once. She lifted herself up and with Teo's assistance the transition from sitting to standing was almost painless. Thankfully he pulled his own hand away immediately once she was upright.

When she saw where they were she gasped again.

'Are you okay? Have you strained something?' He leant in towards her again.

She rubbed her side and nodded. Let him think that, but her wound felt fine. It was the house that had made her gasp. *This* house?

A free-standing two-storey villa in the traditional Spanish style. The windows were shaped like arches and the rooms on the first floor had small balconies overlooking the quiet square.

Most of all it was painted a gorgeous pale pink with orange accents that shouldn't go together but somehow did.

'You live here? *Here?*'

'What's the matter?'

'Nothing,' she whispered. Only everything. It was too strange. She *knew* this house. She'd never been inside, but she'd walked past many times with Pablo and secretly, as she held his hand, imagined what it might be like to live somewhere like that with Pablo.

That was in the brief period where she'd contemplated being that sort of person. The type of person with a house. With a job in the same place every day. A person who owned their own cutlery. And their own sheets. A person who slept in their own bed every night. Even the sort of person who had potted plants.

If she was ever going to do any of those things, she had thought it would be somewhere like this.

Teo lifted her bag from the boot of his car and

walked to the large front door. Wooden, painted a shiny white with two big gold knockers. Gorgeous.

'Have you always lived here?'

'No. Why?'

Of course he hadn't. She'd have known if he'd lived in her dream house, wouldn't she? Besides, Teo had shared a small apartment with Pablo and Val, not far from the university. Not far from her student digs.

She'd never told anyone how much she loved this house. Not even Pablo. Because why would she? Ten years ago, it was beyond the realms of all imagining that either of them would be able to afford a place like this. Besides, she and Pablo were going to travel the world together. What use would a beautiful house in the heart of Old Seville have been to them.

And yet…

Teo pushed open the door and called out, 'We're home.'

She followed him inside to where the cool marble floors and darkness provided a welcome reprieve from the heat. When her eyes adjusted, she noticed the high ceilings, the floor-to-ceiling windows and white curtains that fluttered in the welcome early evening breeze.

A giant staircase loomed above her. Down a corridor, past the staircase, she glimpsed a courtyard and heard the tinkling of a fountain.

The house was even more lovely inside than she'd imagined.

Even before seeing her room she knew Teo was annoyingly right. This place was far nicer than her hotel. Though it remained to be seen whether her host's mood would lose his villa several stars from its rating.

'I'll show you to your room,' he said.

'What if I want to look around first?'

The way his eyebrows shot up let her know he hadn't anticipated this level of sass.

'Unless you need a moment to tidy up down here? Pick up your underwear, dirty clothes and the like.'

His lips were tight but she wasn't sure if it was a grimace or a suppressed grin.

He coughed. 'I have some help. As I said, Alba is my housekeeper. She and her husband live in the garden house and take care of everything. The cleaning, cooking, washing, garden.'

Cara didn't take in much after 'garden house.' It implied not just a garden, which was a luxury in itself, but a whole other building. As though this one were not enough.

Did he live here on his own? She'd just assumed as much because, after all Teo was vastly unpleasant, but he was also, it seemed, quite well off. Someone must think he was a catch.

Not her though. He was grumpy, uptight. Reserved. And not even his sharp jaw and definitive cheekbones could compensate for that. Nor could his height or his broad chest, which she conceded, wasn't nothing. Teo Ortiz was, she had to admit, handsome. Objectively. If you didn't know him and didn't have to take his brittle personality into account.

'Do they know I'll be staying a few days?'

'They know you'll be staying as long as it takes you to recuperate.' Teo stepped towards her, but Cara wasn't sure which direction he was going in and if she was meant to follow. Somehow, they ended up with only a foot of air between them, facing one another. Somehow, her heart was in her throat.

'I'm very grateful for you letting me stay, but how long I stay isn't up to you. I assume you don't propose to lock me up?'

'Of course not. But I do plan on making your stay so comfortable that you'll never want to leave.'

A laugh bubbled up through her, responding to his joke, but when her gaze caught his, her laugh froze. His eyes were dark, but focused on her. He hadn't been joking.

He almost looked serious. The air crackled between them.

'Never? That's quite the challenge you're setting for yourself.' Her voice was rough, but that was surely still the effects of the operation. She wasn't herself.

His voice, on the other hand, was soft and certain as he said, 'I always rise to a challenge. You should know that about me.'

She was certainly getting to.

She knew she should step back; they'd been standing too close to one another for far too long. She could see the weave in his silk tie. The strain in his jaw. But her body was tender and quick movements painful, so she remained where she was.

The sound of a throat being cleared made Teo turn his head. In the second it took Cara to follow she thought she glimpsed a hint of a pink flush climb up Teo's neck.

'Alba, this is Cara. Cara, this is Alba, my housekeeper and general lifesaver.'

'Cara, it's lovely to meet you, I'm sorry it's not under better circumstances. How are you feeling?' Alba asked.

'Thank you. I'm doing fine, all things considered.'

'I've made up your room. It's on this floor as I understand you mustn't climb stairs?'

Had Teo told her that? Or did she just know? Either way Cara's body felt a sense of relief. Walking was an effort. Stairs would take everything out of her.

'You'll also find some new clothes as well, nothing fancy, but I hope you find them comfortable as you convalesce.'

'Oh, you didn't have to. I would've made do.'

As if on cue, Alba glanced at her backpack, still being held effortlessly in Teo's hand.

'That's all you have?' the older woman asked.

'That's all I need.'

Cara braced herself to explain yet again about her lifestyle but Alba simply said, 'Please leave out anything you'd like for me to wash.'

'There's no need…'

Alba's face fell and Teo shot her a look that said, *Do what this woman says.*

'Thank you, I will,' Cara said.

'I'll show you your room,' Teo said.

Cara followed him down a second corridor, away from the inviting courtyard, and towards the back of the house. She'd only turned two corners yet already felt lost. He opened a door to a large room that was dark and cool. Dark was good. A lie-down would be better.

'I imagine you want to rest.'

'Yes, thank you. I do.'

'You have an en suite. And if you need Alba, just pick up the intercom and call for her.'

'I couldn't—'

'You can and you must. Not only is it what I pay her for but she claims she's hopelessly under-employed looking after just me and is delighted to have someone else to fuss over.'

So he did live alone. It made sense. Not even

a face as handsome as his could make up for his cool attitude.

'I won't need anything.'

'Presumably you'll need to eat?'

Yes. But she'd figure that out later. Food was the last thing on her mind. For now, she just wanted to have a reprieve from Teo, his dark eyes and contradictory smiles. And once she'd slept she wouldn't feel so rattled by the way his hand felt wrapped around hers.

He placed her backpack on a sofa, lying it the right way up.

'Do you need help opening it?' he asked.

Why was he being so damned helpful? It was too much. Too strange. Couldn't he see she was in a vulnerable place?

Her backpack contained most of her belongings. Travel light, travel with ease. She shopped at thrift shops, bought clothes made locally in places she visited, though she found she really only needed a handful of good quality outfits. She was acutely aware of her flight miles, but offset those by consuming and purchasing no more than she absolutely needed. One exception she made was earrings. They were light, compact and could transform any outfit into something memorable. Together with a few shades of bright lipstick was all she needed to make her feel special and inject a bit of style into her day. Besides, interpreters were not meant to stand out, her job was to blend in.

'I can manage, really.'

Teo backed towards the door, but didn't leave right away.

'Are you waiting for a tip?' she joked.

His face fell and she felt smaller than she ever had. He might have been rude to her in the past but he was making an effort now. Maybe he was trying to make amends.

'I'm sorry, that was uncalled for. I'm not at my best.'

'It's fine, I understand,' he replied, but he still looked crestfallen as he closed the door behind him.

But why? He didn't like her. He never had, so why was he being so different and helpful and downright contradictory?

It's because of Pablo. He doesn't know how to treat you and having you here might be bringing back sad memories for him as well.

Cara sat on the bed and sighed. She toed off her shoes. On the bed next to her were a pair of long silky pyjamas. Soft under her fingertips. She sighed again and decided it would be worth the effort to feel those against her skin instead of the rough cotton dress she was wearing.

She winced as she unbuttoned her dress, slipped it off and dressed slowly again. She could take more painkillers but needed to eat something when she did and didn't have the energy to deal with Alba, let alone Teo for the moment, but on a table near the window she spied several bottles of water, some sparkling, some still, and a bowl of fruit. Apples, bananas, strawberries. She peeled a banana, opened a bottle of painkillers and obediently took her tablets.

Then she did something she hadn't done before. Looked up Verdadero, the company Teo had established with Pablo and Val. The start-up she had known ten years ago was now a massive company, with so many games and parts of the business she didn't bother to count. Teo and Val weren't simply successful, they were the best in the world and had made Pablo's game into a success so many times over. She closed her eyes and lay on the bed. It was too much to take in: happiness, grief, regret, pride. Tears leaked from her eyes. She'd get under the covers in a bit.

But she fell asleep before she did.

Teo sat under the wisteria, which was in full purple bloom, and swiped through the morning's news on his tablet. He glanced over occasionally at the shutters to the guest room. They remained defiantly shut. He expected nothing else.

His house was clearly the last place on earth Cara wanted to be. It was written all over the smooth skin of her cheek bones, in the wariness in her golden-brown eyes and in the way she held her pink lips tight. *Why would she want to stay here when you've always been cold to her?* Cara really despised him and the passage of time had done nothing to dull that feeling.

Why would it? He had good reason for remaining aloof with her, as much now as then. He had to.

He needed to maintain the distance between them yet he didn't want her to be miserable. He contemplated explaining to her that he had good reasons for maintaining his distance, but that would prompt further questions. Questions he didn't trust her enough to answer. The same old conundrum.

So he stood and moved to the chair on the opposite side of the table, with his back to her room. There. Now maybe he could focus on the stock market and not the door to Cara's room or what the woman behind it was doing.

He poured himself a coffee from the pot Alba had brewed for him. Black. Long. All his stomach could handle for the time being.

Cara's presence in his house was more distracting than he'd anticipated. She brought memories and pain into his life and a sense of uneasiness he couldn't pin down. Distraction was the last thing he needed at the moment, not with the film producers due to arrive in Seville tomorrow.

His house guest wouldn't stay for long and once she left, he'd feel like himself again. While he knew Cara would keep to herself, having anyone he didn't know very well stay under his roof made him uneasy. You just never knew what they were up to or what they would say about him once they left.

People—ex girlfriends mainly—had told him he had a trust problem. Teo didn't see his reluctance to trust people as a problem, more of a solution: If you were cautious about who you let into your life, you had less to worry about. Most people in the world were just far too trusting. And that was where their problems began.

Pablo sprung to mind.

Pablo had fallen hard and fast for Cara. Too hard and way too fast if you asked Teo. And Teo had told Pablo as much. Told him to step back, take a breath. He didn't want to see his best friend hurt. Cara hadn't been the one to hurt Pablo, but that wasn't the point. Falling in love was reckless.

Teo hadn't thought of Cara in years. Not really. Occasionally something would bring her to mind and he'd wonder where she was, what she was doing, whether she had settled down. Not that he *cared*, but he was curious. For Pablo's sake. That was all.

A noise behind him made him swing his head. His body a hair-trigger. He stood.

There she was. Standing on the other side of the courtyard, in loose white pyjamas, her golden hair cascading around her face like a halo. Looking mortified.

'Sorry to interrupt. I didn't realise you were here.'

'Please don't apologise. Think of this house as yours while you're here.'

She raised an eyebrow. He had to get better at sounding sincere.

'Have a seat. Have some coffee. I'm about to leave.' Teo pulled out the chair opposite his.

She looked down. 'You have a full cup. Please just stay,' she said as she sat.

Before he could even ask if Cara was hungry, Alba appeared with a plate of freshly cut fruit and *bollos*, sweet rolls served with jam and butter, as though she'd been spying on him.

You know Alba and you know she definitely was.

His housekeeper had been delighted when Teo had told her they were going to have a house guest. She fussed over Cara, asking how she was feeling, how she had slept. Teo listened in, trying to keep his expression as neutral as possible when Cara said that she had slept well and was feeling much better than the day before.

Alba smiled broadly at Cara and winked at Teo before leaving.

Alba wasn't just a spy but also a meddler.

'This is a beautiful house. How long have you lived here?'

'I bought it about six years ago, but took some time to renovate and repair it. I moved in about five years ago.'

'I'm sorry I was so shocked yesterday. I…' She pressed her lips together. 'I remember this house, that's all.'

'You do?'

'Yes, it's beautiful. Not to mention pink!'

'What's wrong with pink?'

'Nothing. I'm trying to tell you I love it. I remember it from when we were at university.'

He let his shoulders relax a little. He'd always loved this house, its stately air, its location in the corner of the quiet square. The orange trees out the front. He'd loved it since he'd first moved to the centre of Seville as a university student.

'I was lucky it came on the market about the same time I was looking for something.'

It was only half a lie. He'd been looking for something sensible, an apartment suitable for a bachelor. Something low-maintenance. A lock up and leave.

Then he'd seen the realtor sign at the front of this house and he'd known.

He was rarely anything but conservative with his money; his childhood had shaken any recklessness out of him. He almost hadn't bought the house but when he'd taken his mother with him to help him choose a place, they had visited two sensible apartments and here. His mother had told him he'd regret not buying it.

She was right.

Six years later he owned half a dozen of those sensible apartments as sensible investments, but this was his home.

'I used to walk through this square on the way home from classes.'

'Me too. The walk down the avenue was quicker…'

'But not as nice.' She finished his thought.

Their gazes snagged and he smiled before he could stop himself.

'Yes,' he said softly.

They shouldn't think about those days because those memories only led in one tragic direction. So as much as he wanted to keep looking at Cara, trying to decide if her eyes were brown or gold, he looked down and cleared his throat.

'Do you need anything?' he asked.

'Wi-Fi password? I have a little bit of work to do.'

'Work? Aren't you meant to be resting?' He didn't want to tell her what to do but she needed to look after herself.

'I will but I told my client I'd help him find someone to take over my work for the next two weeks.'

'Will that be difficult?' He had no idea what being a freelance interpreter involved, but was always interested how others managed their businesses.

'Yes, interpreters are in high demand. The good ones especially. But I know some people and who to ask.'

'You should charge a finder's fee.'

'Charge my clients for replacing me? When I left them in the lurch?'

He shrugged. 'Yes, a commission.'

'But I'm the one cancelling the work.'

'Will the other interpreters charge as much as you?'

She shook her head.

'Then there you go.'

'No, you don't get it. I can't upset these people, they're my clients. I depend on them for work.'

'And they need you as much as you need them. Think about it. Are you going to freelance forever?'

She opened her mouth as if to say *Yes*, but the word didn't come out.

Interesting.

'What happens if you get sick again? Or can't travel for some reason? How will you earn a living then?'

Her mouth tightened. 'I'll figure out a way.'

'But you don't have a plan.'

Cara put her palms on the table and pushed herself up to standing with a slight groan. He'd gone too far. He was only trying to help but should have seen this was not the brand of assistance Cara would appreciate at all.

'Don't leave, please. I'm sorry if I was out of line. I only want—'

'To criticise my way of life?'

He shook his head. 'No, I'm only trying to help. I'm in awe of your life. It's something I could never do. I don't fully understand it, but I admire it.'

'You've done nothing but berate me since you arrived at the hospital.'

'For that I'm sorry. I feel a kind of responsibility towards you. I know it's misplaced, I know it isn't my right to feel that way, I am sorry for the way I spoke to you at the hospital.'

Cara gripped the wrought iron frame of the chair, but didn't sit.

Let her go. Things will be far easier that way. The tightness in his chest would dissipate for starters.

But he couldn't let her go. He wanted her close. He felt more at ease when he could actually see her. Which was strange. 'Please sit, eat something to get your strength back. I know you are more than capable of organising your affairs, but if there's anything I can do to help you with changing your arrangements, please let me know.'

She pressed her lips together in thought, but then sat again. He exhaled.

Cara rested one of her manicured fingers on

the handle of her coffee cup, but didn't lift it. Her fingers were long and elegant. Unadorned by any jewellery.

'What's on *your* agenda for today?' she countered.

'Work.'

'I figured as much. What are you working on?'

He inhaled deeply through his nose. 'Much like every day.'

'Which is?'

He looked at her, but didn't speak. As a rule, Teo didn't speak much about his work to anyone who wasn't involved in it. You never knew what a person's motives were.

You think Cara's a spy?

Obviously not...

Probably not...

'So it's okay for you to offer me unsolicited advice about how to run my business but you won't even tell me what you do?'

'It's not very interesting.'

She scoffed. 'No, I'm sure being the CEO of a hugely successful tech company is deathly dull. Yes. I looked you up. Verdadero has come a long way since...'

Pablo.

She didn't say it.

Pablo.

'Since you were starting out.'

They had come a long way. Further than any of

them could have imagined. A decade ago, their ambition was simply to design and build a game and find someone willing to buy it. They'd done more than that. Several hundred million people had been willing to buy it along with their subsequent games, making Verdadero's the most popular VR games in the world. Not only that, when they realised the existing engines would not be suitable for the games they wanted to create, Val and his team had developed a whole new one. Gaming architecture that they then licensed to thousands of other developers, meaning Verdadero was one of the most influential and powerful gaming companies in the world.

'You looked us up?'

'You gave me a card? Was I not meant to?'

'No. Of course, I mean…' What did he mean? The sight of Cara, sitting across from him in her practically diaphanous pyjamas was far more disconcerting than it should have been. He struggled to take his eyes off her, and when he studied her soft skin and sparkling eyes, he felt himself losing his grip on his surroundings.

'I'm staying in your house, of course I looked you up.'

And what else had she found out? Had she read about his father? About the scandal that had engulfed his family when he was a child?

As a child, Teo hadn't understood the significance of investment fraud, but as an adult he made sure he knew what it involved and, more importantly, how to avoid it. Along with all the other white-collar and corporate crimes it was possible to commit. No one would ever throw his father's crimes back in his face. And simply the idea that Cara might judge him for them made his shoulders tense.

'You know me,' he said.

She laughed. 'Hardly.'

And he knew she was right.

'Is it some big deal you can't talk about? What you're working on?'

Teo flinched.

'No. I mean, obviously I couldn't tell you if I was.'

'Don't you trust me?' The pain in her voice landed heavily in his chest.

'I don't trust anyone. It isn't personal.'

'I get not trusting others, believe me, but I just asked what you're doing today. I expected you'd say something along the lines of, "I'm going into the office," or "I have a few meetings." I'm not asking for all your passwords.'

He closed his eyes and grounded himself with some deep breaths. She was right. He should just be able to give a casual answer to a casual question. And yet…

'When it comes to business deals, I'm very cautious. I have to be. It's how we made the company into the success it is.'

She snorted. 'I'm hardly going to—'

'I don't for a moment think you would—'

'But?'

'People talk. It can happen unintentionally.'

'Okay, so you're working on a secret deal. Got it.'

As he finished speaking Alba returned to the courtyard.

Thank you, Alba for your impeccable timing. Remind me to give you a raise.

'Will Cara be joining you for dinner tomorrow evening?' Alba asked.

Teo dismissed any thought of giving Alba a raise.

Cara's eyes widened and her gaze flashed from Alba, back to him.

Damn. He still hadn't figured out what to do about the meal he was hosting with the film producers. He'd half contemplated moving the meeting to a nearby restaurant, but it was not his preference to do that as he wanted to discuss business. Val couldn't organise a business dinner to save the company.

Teo didn't want to disturb Cara either.

'I'm hosting a business dinner tomorrow evening. Just a small thing, there'll be four of us.'

'Five, counting Cara,' Alba added.

He really did need to have a word to his overeager housekeeper about minding her own business.

'You don't have to join us,' he said. 'I know you're recuperating.'

'You want me to hide in my room?'

Cara isn't a stranger.

'No. Of course not. I don't want you to feel pressure to join us, if you're tired, or if you simply don't want to.'

'Who'll be coming?'

Alba smiled to herself as she stepped away.

'Val. And two business associates.'

'Val? Oh! How is he?' Cara pressed her hand to her chest. 'I'd love to see him.'

Of course she would. There was no getting out of her coming to dinner now.

'What's the dinner for?'

'To discuss the project we're working on.'

'Ah, the secret project. No wonder you don't want me there.'

'It isn't that I don't want you there, but yes, it is a sensitive and confidential project.'

'It's okay, I don't have to come. But I can keep secrets. I'm an interpreter. If I told you half the deals I've worked on, I'd have to kill you. In fact, I'd wager I've been privy to far more top secret negotiations than you have.'

Shame welled up in him. Not only was Cara not a stranger, she was also a professional. Val would never forgive him if he made Cara stay in her room.

'I'll double-check with Val, but I'm sure it

will be okay if you join us for dinner.' He stood. 'Please rest, your main priority is getting better. There's no need to decide now about tomorrow night.'

'I'd like to see Val very much. But I promise I'll leave you to your secret business dealings.'

Teo walked away with a heaviness coming down on him. Cara was a professional, she'd been at business and political meetings more important than this one, his head knew he could trust her.

Yet his heart? His heart wanted her to leave as soon as possible. Cara only brought trouble. And trouble was difficult to ignore when it sat in your courtyard wearing thin, soft pyjamas.

CHAPTER FOUR

CARA WATCHED TEO stride back into his house, tall, taut and annoyed about so many things.

He really didn't like her. And he really didn't want her there. And yet something about both those things sparked a challenge in her. *Why* didn't he like her? What had she ever done to him? Apart from loving his best friend, which as far as she was aware was not a capital offence, she hadn't done anything.

Whether it was logical or not she owed it to Pablo to make things right between her and Pablo's oldest friend. He'd hate the idea that the two of them were not getting along. The sounds and smells of Seville brought back so many memories of Pablo, of his big eyes, open demeanour, curiosity about the world and everything in it. Pablo adored Teo, so Teo couldn't be that bad, could he?

Back in her room, Cara turned to her backpack, still lying on the sofa where Teo had left it the day before. She might as well unpack and make herself comfortable. He wanted her to stay as long as she needed and maybe she'd been too rash to try to limit her stay. Especially now she knew what a beautiful house Teo lived in. And now she knew that his housekeeper was the lovely Alba. She felt she could relax here. She may be able to stay a while longer. The fact that she'd be annoying Teo was reason enough.

She unzipped her bag fully and placed her clothes neatly in a pile on the sofa beside it. Her suits, her jeans, T-shirts and then the few dresses she owned. She settled on one of her black jersey dresses, the one that came to just above the knee. She wore it to professional functions and it would be just the thing for tomorrow night, which was a business dinner first and foremost.

Even if for her it was a reunion of sorts.

Val.

She placed her hand on her heart. That was why she'd agreed. Curiosity to see Val again. Val, at least, had always liked her. If only the hospital had been put through to Val in the first place.

Fate had a dark sense of humour. One she'd been on the wrong end of many times. Losing the only man she'd ever loved, watching both her parents slip away. Her half-brother's betrayal. She still grieved them, but at least now she knew her fate. She'd already lost everyone it was possible to lose and had no intention of ever letting someone into her heart again.

Yes, fate's sense of humour was very dark indeed.

And now it had sent her to Teo. Grumpy, disapproving, uptight Teo.

What happens if you get sick again? Or can't travel for some reason? How will you earn a living then?

If someone had asked her that even a week ago, she would have told them to mind their own business but the events of the last few days had made her feel exposed for the first time in years. The fact that she had little choice but to stay here with Teo in her current predicament only increased her feelings of vulnerability.

There was a knock at her door. Teo?

She opened the door with her heart in her throat. But it wasn't Teo. It was Alba.

'I've come to see if you would like me to do some washing for you.'

'I…' Her first instinct was to say no. She took care of herself, she always did, but her body ached and Alba seemed so eager. 'Thank you, that would be lovely.'

Cara walked to the sofa where her things lay spread out, but Alba waved her away. It usually felt odd to trust someone with her things and yet with Alba it didn't.

How could it be that she already trusted this woman and yet still struggled with Alba's boss, who she had known for much longer?

'How long have you worked for Teo?' Cara asked.

'Oh, about five years, since he moved into this house.'

Alba pointed to the black dress on the top of the pile. 'Are you wearing this tomorrow night?'

'Yes,' Cara said with a smile.

Alba draped the dress over her arm. 'I'll press it for you.'

'Thank you. And he's a good boss?'

'He's a wonderful boss. Yes.'

Of course an employee would say that. The place was probably bugged.

'Is he still here?'

'No, he's gone to his office. He probably won't be back until this evening. He works too hard. I can't remember the last time he stopped for a siesta.'

Cara shrugged. 'It's hard these days to take that time, I guess.' She was partial to a nap in the afternoon but modern work patterns made that next to impossible.

'Does he host many dinners here?'

'Sometimes, yes. Especially important ones.'

'And tomorrow night is important?'

'Oh yes, very.'

'Why?' Cara was aware she was pushing Alba too much but Teo had been so secretive about it all. It would help everyone if she had some clue what the meeting was about, if only so she didn't put her foot in it.

But Alba wasn't falling for it and somehow it made Cara only like her even more. 'I wish he had a hostess to help him with these things. He'd be so much happier if he had someone by his side.'

Cara doubted if anything or anyone could make Teo happy.

'Oh, Teo and I aren't…we're just…' *Friends* wasn't right. They were forced to be together due to a loyalty they owed to a long dead friend. They were friends once removed. 'Acquaintances.'

'You were friends with Pablo. Good friends,' Alba said. It wasn't a question.

'Yes.' Cara sat on the edge of the bed, the air knocked out of her as it was every time someone said his name. 'Did you know him?'

'Oh no. I didn't know Teo at all before I came to work for him, but I've heard all about Pablo.'

Cara hesitated before asking her next question. She longed to talk about Pablo. After leaving Seville she hadn't been in contact with anyone who knew him. At first that had been good, what she needed for healing. But as the years went by, she wasn't sure. She contemplated getting in touch with Pablo's parents, but she'd left it so many years since she'd last spoken to them that it didn't feel right. So, instead, Pablo was just a memory, something she kept locked away in her heart. Like her memories of her parents. No photos, no mementos. Nothing physical to carry around and weigh her down. Life was easier that way. Lighter.

But being back in Seville, the temptation to think about Pablo was too much.

'What have they told you?'

'Oh dear, you knew him, not I. I know he was remarkable. A gifted artist. And storyteller. I know his friends loved him dearly.'

Cara nodded.

That was all true. And it was enough.

Pablo also made her laugh, made her feel safe. He made her world whole. He made her see the world in a whole new, brighter light. She felt safe with him, loved. She hadn't felt that way since.

Cara cleared her throat. 'I don't know Teo as well. We haven't actually spoken since…well. You know. He lives here all alone?'

Alba smiled knowingly. Cara didn't care; she suspected that her knowledge of Teo's love life was the one confidence Alba might be willing to break.

'Yes, apart from Geraldo, my husband, and I.'

'No girlfriends?'

'Not to my knowledge and I know him pretty well.'

Alba washed his sheets, did his laundry. If anyone knew about Teo's love life, she would.

'Why not, do you think?'

Alba laughed now. 'Careful, you might cause me to breach my housekeeper privilege.'

'I'm sorry, I'm just… I'm curious. I don't understand him at all. The only thing I know is that he doesn't like me very much.'

It was a relief to say that out loud. It somehow lost some of its power.

Alba's brow furrowed. 'He'd hardly ask you to stay if he didn't like you.'

'He feels as though he owes it to Pablo. That's all.'

'Pish. That's not it at all. He could have just paid someone to look after you elsewhere if he didn't want you to stay. He's a very wealthy man.'

It was a good point. If Teo didn't like her, if he couldn't stand the sight of her, there were other options. He'd opened his home to her.

You don't need to understand him; you just need to accept his hospitality.

'You look tired, you should lie down. When you're hungry, let me know.'

Yes, rest was a good thing. Her body only seemed to have a few hours of energy to spare before she needed to be horizontal again. Alba closed the shutters and left Cara to rest. It was nice, she decided, letting someone take care of her for a change. It was nice being looked after. She was glad she had agreed to come.

Even though she'd never admit that to Teo. Not in a million years.

* * *

It was hours later when she woke. Alba had washed and ironed the entire contents of her backpack and everything was now hanging straight and pressed in the clean-smelling wardrobe. Even her backpack, her trusty, reliable friend, looked and smelt as though it had had a clean as well.

She mustn't let herself get used to this.

In a week or two she'd be back on the road doing her own laundry.

As though she had a camera in her room, Alba knocked on the bedroom door and came in with a tray of food, which she placed on the small table.

'How are you feeling?'

'Still tired, but maybe a little better.'

'Have some lunch. It's a bean soup I make for Geraldo when he's not well. There's more in the fridge anytime you want to help yourself. Along with some other things.'

Cara didn't think she'd ever have the opportunity to help herself to anything, given Alba's attentiveness.

She went through her emails as she ate and was relieved to see a message from a fellow interpreter, Leanne, agreeing to take on not only the job for Mr Westwood, but the work Cara had scheduled in Paris for the week after next.

Relieved, but still disappointed. Almost four weeks' worth of work lost just like that. Teo's suggestion that she charge her client a finder's fee wasn't a totally foolish idea. Many people did do that. Agencies did that. But she wasn't an agency. She was a freelancer.

Yet, you found Leanne, you are vouching for her. Leanne is happy, the clients are happy. Cara had many years' experience. She had contacts all over the world in business, politics and law. And she knew many interpreters. She'd be ideally placed to set up her own agency.

No. Just the idea of what all that might involve overwhelmed her. She knew nothing about starting up a business. She closed her laptop and set it down on the bed next to her. Exhausted, she lay down. Even though it would only be for a short time, it was nice being looked after for a change. To feel safe. She was soon asleep again.

The following evening, Teo showered and changed into a fresh outfit. Trousers, white shirt and a jacket. No tie—he wanted to appear casual. He hadn't seen Cara since the morning prior, as she'd kept to her room, but Alba had informed him that Cara was feeling fine but resting. Alba had passed on the message from Teo that Val would love to see her at this evening's dinner.

He went downstairs, even though it was only eight thirty and the guests would not arrive until nine. Alba had set everything out and there was nothing left to do, which was a shame because if he had something to do with his hands, he was sure he'd feel much better. He had nothing to do but pace the living room.

He didn't usually feel like this before a business dinner. He'd done big deals before. Arguably bigger deals. And if this fell through there would be others.

It isn't the deal. You know it isn't.

It was the woman who had been staying in his guest room for the past few days.

And there she was, as though he had conjured her, standing in the doorway, barefoot, wearing a black dress that clung to her curves like a lover and showed off her hourglass figure to perfection.

'Good evening,' he said and realised his mouth had turned suddenly and unexpectedly dry.

'I'm sorry, I was looking for Alba.'

'She's preparing dinner. Can I help you with anything?'

'Um. I…'

'What is it?'

'It's my dress. There are buttons at the back I can't reach because I can't lift my arms.'

'Oh.' His heart leapt. That would be a better job for Alba but he said, 'I can help,' before he could think better of it.

'Are you sure?'

'Of course, it's not a problem.'

Of course it wasn't a problem. Why would standing right behind her and placing his hands next to the soft skin of Cara's neck and back be a problem?

Because somehow any activity that involved him being within a breath of Cara seemed to be a problem. Dry mouth. Trembling fingers. Completely irrational reactions.

She hates you, remember? She's Pablo's girlfriend, remember?

He walked slowly towards her, each step heavier than the next. She turned her back to him, tried to lift her hand to move her thick mane of hair out of the way but winced.

'I'm sorry but it hurts to lift my arms.'

'May I?'

She nodded and Teo braced himself before using one hand to push her hair to one side, thick, heavy and so much softer than seemed possible. He wanted to slide his fingers into it, feel the silkiness down the length of his fingers, but he shook the impulse away. He had to concentrate on the buttons, but looking down he was perplexed by the puzzle facing him. The dress was wide open, exposing all the creamy skin of Cara's back. A large lump formed in his stomach as his gaze travelled up and down her spine. This was far more than he'd anticipated.

It took him an age to actually locate the buttons hidden in the folds of the fabric. When he pulled the two halves of the back of the dress together, he saw that once the buttons were fastened they would create a large circle in the back of the dress. No. Not a circle. But a love heart against the smooth skin of her back. He gulped.

His fingers did not feel like his own and he struggled to grasp the delicate buttons without brushing his own fingers against the soft skin of Cara's neck. Her shoulders stiffened and she stood straighter, causing him to lose his grip on the small pearl-like buttons entirely. He began the Herculean task again, but the sight of her creamy skin was too distracting, the wisps of hair that kept falling back over his hands ticklish, the small divot behind her ear hypnotising. Not to mention her perfume, swirling around him like a spell. Three tiny buttons, three even smaller holes. He'd never been this close to her before, never touched her, but it shouldn't be this difficult. His fingers shouldn't feel so numb and useless. As he finally got the last button through, he sighed with relief.

They were the longest three buttons of his life.

It's just Cara, Pablo's out-of-reach girlfriend.

Ex-girlfriend? Was that the term? She wasn't a widow either.

Either way, it was a ridiculous reaction to be having. He didn't react like this to women as a rule. He usually managed to keep the distance he knew he had to, physically and emotionally. He never let himself get too close until he could be absolutely sure that he could trust them.

'How are you feeling?' he asked, praying she didn't ask the same question of him.

'I'm okay. I slept most of the day again.'

'Good.' She was on the mend and it was a relief.

Cara stepped back. Her feet were bare and he noticed a small tattoo on one of them that looked like a green sea-turtle. Apart from her feet, she was dressed and made up for an evening out. She was exquisite. His throat tightened. He swallowed but felt no relief. Tonight was happening, whether he was ready for it or not. He had to trust her. He at least had to let her in.

'I should probably explain what tonight is about,' he said.

'Only if you want to. I am very discreet. I am also happy to sign an NDA.'

'You are?'

'Of course, it's standard practice in my line of work.'

Teo felt the skin on his cheeks burn. He was being ridiculous. Cara was a professional, even though she was not here in a professional capacity, she still had a reputation to protect. One she could destroy if she leaked any details of tonight's meeting.

'That won't be necessary. I trust you.' The words felt strange on his tongue. Unfamiliar.

'Maybe you could start by telling me who your other guests this evening will be?'

'Val, of course. And two men interested in developing a project with us.'

'Another game?'

'No. Something different. A movie. They're from a Hollywood studio.'

Cara's eyes opened wider than he'd ever seen them. Gold. Definitely gold with hints of brown.

'Wow, that's huge.'

'It is.'

'Which game?'

'*Matador*.' Again his tongue was too big for his mouth. Would she recognise that as Pablo's game? Their first game?

She nodded but didn't speak. He had his answer.

'I didn't mean to be rude about you attending tonight. It is a business meeting first and foremost.'

She shook her head. 'It's okay.'

'It's a big deal for us. Not just financially, but because we want to make sure that the people we choose to make this movie with are the right people. That they'll respect the intent of the game, its essence.'

'Yes, of course. You want to make sure they do it right.'

Because of Pablo, he thought, though neither of them said that.

'I'd better finish getting ready,' she said.

'You already look beautiful.'

He was as shocked by his remark as she looked. He hadn't meant to think it, let alone say it. For the longest second, they both stood, frozen, staring at one another.

Her golden eyes were wide open and her jaw slack. Apparently, she couldn't believe what he'd said either. A giggle burst out of her. She almost sounded nervous. 'Shoes would be good though. I don't want them to think I'm a complete heathen.' She spun and left before he could respond. His heart still in his throat.

What had just happened?

He knew what. He knew that his main mission for this evening had changed. He should be focused on the deal, on the producers, but instead his main aim would be to keep his thoughts away from Cara. On the way her hair felt in his fingers. On the colour of her eyes. Gold? Brown? Amber? If he could manage to do that, the evening might not be a failure.

His last glimpse of Cara leaving the room, her long strawberry-blonde hair swishing against her back, hiding the large love heart in the back of her dress that he now knew was there. That no one else would know about but that he wouldn't be able to keep his thoughts away from.

That and the tattoo on her foot. The little turtle.

A turtle? Why would she mark her body permanently with a turtle?

For the first time since seeing her in the hospital Teo decided it wouldn't be such a bad thing if Cara cut her stay with him short.

You're going to push her out onto the street if she's not better?

Pablo wouldn't want that.

Yeah, but Pablo also wouldn't want Teo getting all tingly over a few buttons. Pablo wouldn't want Teo's mouth drying up at the sight of the skin on Cara's back and neck. Pablo, who had trusted him with his games and his legacy.

Pablo would probably tell Teo to put Cara up in a hotel if he knew about the unwanted and unbidden thoughts that were managing to creep their way into Teo's head. No one must know about those thoughts. Teo must only acknowledge them long enough to push them far, far away. Under lock and key.

CHAPTER FIVE

CARA'S NECK CONTINUED to tingle at the memory of Teo's fingertips brushing the sensitive skin on the nape of her neck. Rough against smooth, cool yet scorching. Light and feathery and discombobulating. Even after her recent abdominal surgery, she'd trembled with awareness when Teo had touched the small spot on the back of her neck. The warmth had fanned out down her spine.

He was anxious about this evening and the deal, that was all. She was looking forward to seeing Val again. No wonder the air around them was charged.

Back in her room, she slipped on a pair of black sandals and applied her signature red lipstick. Then she sat and waited until it was closer to nine and the time for the arrival of the guests. Enough time for doubt to creep in. Why had she agreed to this? Teo was right, she was better off staying in her room. She wasn't well, as shown by the fact her heart was racing at a simple touch from Teo.

But she'd wanted to prove Teo wrong. To find out his secret. She'd wanted to get the better of him.

And now she knew his secret—and it was a good one. A movie deal! That was huge. For Teo and for Verdadero.

Matador.

That had been Pablo's game. And now it might become a movie. The emotions that rocked her were complex: pride that something Pablo had created had been so successful, sadness that he would never see it. Gratitude to Teo and Val for making it such a success. For honouring Pablo in such a way. Teo might have been unfriendly to her but he was still a good friend.

Mateo Ortiz, confusing as always.

When she returned to the living room, Teo was standing with a familiar-looking figure. His hair was shorter than the last time she'd seen him but she would know him anywhere.

Val.

'Cara! Cara! It's been too long. How are you? Can I hug you or are you too sore?'

She laughed. 'Gently, and yes.'

Val stepped towards her and she anticipated the sensation of his body touching hers. Would it scorch her like Teo's had? Val wrapped his arms around her and she fell easily into them. It was nice, comforting, but her heart rate remained steady.

Interesting.

'It's so lovely to see you,' she said, stepping back to look at him. 'You haven't changed one bit.'

'But you have. You are even more beautiful.'

They both laughed at his compliment. Things with Val had always been easy, even brotherly. No sparks. Confusion. No annoyance, only smiles. No dark looks like the one Teo was giving them now.

The two producers arrived not long after. One American, one British. Both older than Teo and Val, who were in their early thirties, but not significantly. They greeted Cara with a puzzled look but their faces brightened when she greeted them in English with her American accent. The Spaniards spoke good English, but speaking other languages was Cara's job, as was mediating between people so smoothly that no one even noticed her presence.

Teo introduced Cara as an old friend of his and Val's who was staying with him for a while. He didn't mention her operation, for which she was grateful. She was easily welcomed as part of their party.

While Teo got the two men drinks, Val took her aside and picked up her hand.

'I'm so sorry you're here under such circumstances, but it really is lovely to see you.'

'You too, Val, it's been too long. And that's been on me.'

'Nonsense, it's on all of us. We've been busy.'

'It was just easier…' She faltered and he squeezed her hand.

'I understand and I suppose you've been reminiscing about Pablo with Teo. I don't want to bring it all up again.'

She shook her head. 'No. We haven't talked about him much. Or, actually, at all.' Now she came to think about it, she'd been doing a lot of thinking about Pablo, but she'd never spoken his name and nor had Teo.

'He hasn't mentioned him. What? Not at all?'

Cara shook her head. 'No. Not directly.' Though his presence hung heavily over both of them.

Val pulled a face and then looked over to Teo, who was passing one man a beer and the other a wine. 'Interesting,' he said.

Though Cara didn't find it the least bit interesting. It was part of Teo being aloof and distant with her. They didn't share personal feelings with one another. That was how it was with them.

The evening went more smoothly than she'd anticipated, and she wondered what Teo had been concerned about. Teo and Val spoke some English and the American man knew some Spanish. If Cara hadn't been there the four of them would have managed, but she naturally fell into the role of a semi-formal interpreter and filled in all the gaps in the conversation. They spoke less about business than she had anticipated, but more about general topics, their lives, families and hobbies. It wasn't exactly like working, but not unlike it either.

Alba brought them their food, a large spread of tapas dishes that she laid out on the table in front of them, including garlicky shrimp, empanadas, pork belly *pintxos* and chorizo croquettes. Cara ate more than she had in days.

Alba whispered to Cara, 'I will be leaving now for the evening, Teo knows this, so don't even think about clearing this away, I will do it in the morning.' Then she placed her hand on Cara's shoulder and whispered, 'It's good to see you looking so well.'

Cara's heart warmed, Alba had been such a support. When she turned back to the table, she caught Teo looking at her and for once he wasn't frowning. His face was relaxed, almost wistful. The frown lines had vanished and his eyes were bright.

Cara's throat turned dry and she reached for the carafe that held the water but at the same instant Teo did as well. Their fingers brushed as they both pulled their hands sharply away. The spark she felt brought back the memory of the buttons and the heat zipping up and down her back. Judging by the way Teo blinked and flinched he felt it too.

'Sorry,' he said and smiled, before taking the carafe and filling her glass.

It was so lovely when he smiled. Which he hardly ever did at her.

When he smiled his whole demeanour brightened and she found it difficult to pull her eyes away from him.

He doesn't like you, he never has. You don't care how handsome he might be.

It might have been the mood or the glass of wine she allowed herself but Cara began to relax. She had made the right decision to join the men; it was a nice evening.

She had a long talk with the American man, Jerry, about his family and then a chat with Val about all the things they had both been doing since they last saw one another. Val gave her the potted history of how they had built their business, from launching their first game, then deciding to develop their own gaming engine and branching out into VR hardware.

After Pablo's passing, they had used many of his story ideas but brought in others to help develop them. Val's technical brain and Teo's drive had made the company grow larger and larger. Cara could see from Teo's house that they were doing well, but she hadn't really turned her mind to how well they must have been doing until she heard Jerry describe Verdadero as 'The most impressive gaming software company in the world.'

She was so pleased for them. These men were only boys when she first met them, just starting out and fumbling around.

And then it came, the sadness that hit her in the chest and then radiated out into the rest of her.

Pablo should have been here too.

She was in the middle of a conversation with Jerry, so she couldn't just stand up and leave, but that was what she wanted to do. Get up and run back to her room and sob and sob.

She was no stranger to this feeling, it hit her at all sorts of inconvenient times and places, and it was not just about Pablo, but something would often bring her parents to mind and she would have to let the feelings sit where they were, breathe deeply and wait until they subsided, as she did now.

She'd become practised at letting the feelings not overwhelm her. As she did now.

She was barely thirty but had already dealt with a lifetime of grief. She refused to let it stop her; her parents and Pablo would have wanted her to live her life. So she got on with things, to honour them, but that didn't mean that sometimes it all didn't catch up with her. She could only be so strong. And she knew she'd never be strong enough to let anyone into her heart again. It was the only way she knew to cope.

Teo leant in her direction and whispered, 'How are you feeling?'

She looked at her watch rather than meet his eyes. He placed his hand over hers and her breath caught. It was so natural to touch him, it felt so right. And yet her thoughts still swirled with Pablo and she took her hand away.

'It's getting late,' he said. 'You should leave if you wish.'

Even though Teo had been subtle, the other men also looked at their watches and the evening began to wind down, with promises to finalise their dealings the next day.

It had been a success and she was glad to have helped. Whatever else Teo was, he was a good host and taking very good care of her.

As Val bid her good evening he asked, 'Will you stay for the ball?'

'What ball?' Cara looked from Val to Teo and back again.

'The tenth anniversary ball,' Val said as though it was obvious.

It was not the tenth anniversary of the business. She knew that. Or of Pablo's death. Besides that was hardly something to be celebrated.

'Of the Pablo Pascal Foundation,' Val said.

What? She'd never heard of a charity named after Pablo.

That's because you've been actively avoiding anything to do with Pablo or Seville. Because when she did it lead to the very feeling she was having now, tightness in her chest and pressure behind her eyes.

Going to such a ball felt like too much so she simply shook her head.

'That's a shame. It would have been so fitting to have you there.'

She caught the look that passed between Teo and Val: a sharp warning from Teo and a puzzled frown from Val.

What didn't she know?

Once everyone left the house and he had closed the door behind them, Teo turned to Cara and his breath caught. Again.

Hopefully this new reaction to her presence was just a temporary thing. *It'll disappear after a proper night's sleep. It's just the stress of the dinner and the deal. The strangeness of having someone else sleep under your roof.*

'I'm sorry it's so late and we kept you up.'

Cara smiled and his breath caught again. She looked bright and she was smiling at him.

It was as though something had unhooked in his shoulders. He'd trusted her, he'd let her in and not only had the sky not fallen but the evening had been a resounding success. It hardly made sense to him.

'It's fine. I've been sleeping so much the past few days. It was good to be around people.'

'Thank you for tonight you were...' Wonderful. Heavenly. Cara's presence had meant that the evening had gone even better than he'd hoped. It had been more of a relaxed social event than tense business deal. They had all got to know and understand one another a little more and that always made doing business so much easier. 'Great, really great. It was really good to have you join us.'

An understatement. He and Val would have plodded on with their adequate English, but Cara brought an easiness, a fluency to the whole evening that none of the men on their own could have managed. And she connected with the producers on a level that was far more personal than he and Val ever would have on their own.

He expected her to turn and leave for the night but instead she said, 'Tell me about the foundation.'

'It's a charity. Val and I set up after…' Under most circumstances he loved talking about the Pablo Pascal Foundation. But this was Cara. And this was a conversation topic that would lead to Pablo. The one thing he didn't want to speak about with her. Talking to Cara was tricky enough, but talking with her about Pablo? That just seemed too much. They both missed him so deeply, and yet their relationships with him had been so different, even contrary at times.

Cara and Pablo had loved one another, pure and simple. Teo's relationship with Pablo wasn't as simple, Pablo had been the first person outside Teo's family to welcome Teo after his father's disgrace. More than that, without Pablo's creations, Teo could not have built Verdadero. Without Pablo, Teo wouldn't be a success.

'That's wonderful. Is it a fundraising ball?'

'Not exactly. We don't tend to fundraise. It's an event we give to thank our patrons and the people who work with us.'

'How do you raise the money for the charity if you don't fundraise?' she asked.

'One-third of all the profits of the business go to the charity.'

She gasped. 'One-third? You donate one-third of your business to charity? But that must be...'

Billions of euros, yes.

His spine straightened. 'Yes, we do. Do you have a problem with that?'

'No! I'm just shocked. You give away a *third* of your earnings?'

He'd heard this before many times, especially when they were first starting out. Not long after Pablo's passing. Investors, banks, all thought they were mad to be doing that from the outset. *You're giving away a third of your money when you could be reinvesting it? Don't you realise how foolish that is?*

'I wouldn't put it like that. I've never considered that money to be mine.'

'Why not?'

He shook his head, but didn't have to speak.

She answered her own question. 'Because it's Pablo's. One-third is Pablo's share. Is that it?'

Teo looked down. He was so proud of the foundation. And he was tired of people doubting their decision to divert Pablo's share of the profits into the charity. He thought Cara, of all people, would agree with it. Bracing himself, he looked her in the eye. 'We have permission from Pablo's family. They're happy for us to be doing this.'

Cara clenched her fists together, as though she were angry about something.

And then he realised.

'If you think that you might be entitled to some of that money, then by all means, we can discuss the matter.'

'What on earth are you talking about?' She spoke slowly and his heart fell. She was furious.

'That's what you're getting at, isn't it? That it's Pablo's money and you're wondering if you're entitled to any of it?'

'You think I'm after the money?' she spat.

Okay, that was *not* what she meant.

Cara's face was white and he was torn between resolving this misunderstanding and getting her to sit down, lest she fell.

'How could you even think such a thing?' Cara's eyes were wide.

'You seemed angry.'

'I certainly am now!'

'Are you okay? Should you sit down?'

'Don't tell me to sit. How dare you! How dare you even think that I'd want Pablo's money.'

'I…ah…that's not… I mean…'

Be quiet, Teo. You're only making things worse. He wasn't usually lost for words but when it came to Cara the ground beneath him often felt unsteady.

'I'd only been seeing him for a little while.'

Cara clenched her fists even tighter.

She's not angry, she's just upset. Really upset.

'I didn't love him because of his money! I loved him because he was him.'

And finally, Teo understood.

He was the fool.

'I cannot believe you, Teo. After everything. After what you've seen of me in the past few days, do you honestly think I'm trying to get my hands on part of this business? Do you honestly think I'm trying to take a cent away from the charity? I was simply amazed that you would be so generous.'

Ah. That was it.

'You seemed so upset.'

'The only thing I'm upset about is that you seem to think I'm some sort of stealthy gold-digger. Does anything you've learned about me suggest the money means anything to me? Or possessions? I don't need anything I can't earn myself. And I certainly don't need money destined for a charity.' She blinked back tears. 'I think it's best if I find a hotel. It's too late now, but I'll leave first thing in the morning.'

No. She mustn't leave.

'Cara, you don't have to.'

'Clearly, I do. You've got some weird misconception in your head about who and what I am, yet the stupid thing, Teo, is that you don't know the first thing about me. You've never even tried to get to know me. You made your mind up about me from the start. I told myself I didn't care what you thought of me, that it didn't matter, but just now you were so far out of line I don't think I can stand to spend even one more night under the same roof as you.'

Cara turned and left the room. He knew he should stop her but he was rooted to the spot. Besides, if he spoke he was only bound to make things worse than they already were. Why couldn't he just speak to her like a normal person? Why did he always have to think the worst of other people? Especially Cara.

Teo lifted a cushion from the sofa, pressed it to his face and screamed.

He was a normal person, wasn't he? A normal, functioning human who had never had such difficultly with any other person. Why couldn't he just get his act together around Cara? She had never been the enemy.

He hated himself at that moment. Even for

thinking she was after Pablo's share of the business, much less saying it out loud.

Because the crazy thing was, he didn't think that at all about her. Not for a second. Oh, how he wanted something to dislike about her, because then everything about this situation would be so much simpler. But the harder he looked for something to dislike about Cara, the more he liked her. And the worse he felt. He couldn't like her. He couldn't be attracted to her. He couldn't feel sparks when he touched her. He just couldn't.

The sound of a throat being cleared forced him to remove the pillow from his face.

Just when he thought the evening couldn't get any worse, it just had.

'Are you okay?' she asked, but there was an edge to her voice.

'I'm fine.'

'That's why you were screaming into a cushion.'

'I always do that when I'm happy.'

And the strangest thing happened. She laughed. Not just a scoff, but a loud, deep laugh, straight from her belly. Which she then clutched with her arms. 'Ouch, don't make me laugh. It still hurts.'

'I'm sorry,' he said.

'Teo, you're messed-up. You know that don't you?'

It wasn't a joke, she was serious. And so was he when he replied, 'I assure you I do. I am so sorry. There was no excuse for what I implied before. None at all. I apologise profusely. If you want to leave my house, I wouldn't blame you but please don't, I will leave myself. Alba can look after you for as long as you need and I'll go to a hotel. Please don't leave because I was unspeakably rude.'

She stood still and calm, staring at him, contemplating her next move.

'I just don't understand you,' she said.

'*I* don't understand me.'

'That's not an excuse, Teo. You're a grown man and clearly competent. Tonight, you were negotiating a multimillion-dollar movie deal. You're not a fool.'

But when it came to her it seemed as though he was.

'I don't know how to behave around you,' he admitted.

There it was honest. And maybe too revealing.

'Why on earth not?'

'Because of Pablo.'

There. He'd said it. Said his name. And surprisingly the earth hadn't opened up. 'Because Pablo is still such an important part of my life and you loved Pablo and because I loved Pablo and I…'

That was a sentence he couldn't finish because it would prove once and for all that he was as petty and mean as he was afraid he was. And she'd yell at him again.

Because Pablo was my friend and I shouldn't have these thoughts about you. I shouldn't be imagining what it is like to touch you. To kiss you...

No. His emotions were on him. He needed to deal with his feelings and it wasn't her fault.

She just nodded. 'Yes, I see. I miss him too. I always will.' She pressed her palm to her heart. 'But instead of being all weird around me, can't you just relax? I'm not going to fall apart when I speak about him, I promise. It was a long time ago.'

She was right; she had spoken to Val about Pablo several times this evening. He'd even heard her laughing when she did.

'You don't miss him?'

'Of course I do, but I deal with it. Yes, it's hard being back here, in Seville, but I'm honestly alright. We can talk about him, you know.'

She was more generous than she needed to be and he nodded.

'And besides, can you imagine what Pablo would say to you right now? "What on earth do you think you're doing, amigo?"'

Teo's lips twitched. Yes, that is exactly what Pablo would have said.

'And he'd probably have hit me on the back of the head.'

Cara laughed again and it vibrated in his chest.

He wanted to hear the sound again, like his new favourite song.

'Yes, he would've. He'd be horrified to know that we aren't getting along. And sad.'

Teo's gut clenched. Pablo would be upset. Devastated.

He'd be more devastated if he knew that you are wondering what it would be like to step up to Cara now and slide your hand into her hair and tilt her lips towards yours.

'I promise to do better. I find it hard to talk about him. And having you here, it's…' He didn't finish the sentence. He couldn't, because by that point Cara was next to him, placing her hand on his forearm and his entire body froze. Waiting. For what might happen next.

'It's okay, we don't have to talk about him if you don't want to. But I'm not going to fall apart. I'm okay,' she said.

Needing to breathe, Teo stepped back and her hand fell.

'I thought you'd gone to bed.'

'I did, then I remembered the buttons.'

The blasted buttons. She turned her back and he steeled himself before he got close to her again. He placed his hand against the shock of her golden hair and moved it aside as slowly as he dared, letting the silky waves wash over his knuckles. His fingers shook as he slipped one button through the loop and then the next. He wasn't faking difficulty, he was trying as hard as he could not to make contact with her skin. He didn't need that kind of confusing torture. Not now. Not after everything that had just happened. Yet the buttons were so small, the loops they had to go through even smaller. Even with the best of intentions, his knuckles still scraped across the tender skin of her neck. He still felt the silkiness against his own skin, every pore on high alert.

As soon as he released the last button he said, 'I'm truly sorry about before. I miss him. And sometimes I don't know what to do. And seeing you again…it's brought a whole lot of things back up.' That wasn't a lie. It was perhaps the most honest thing he'd said to her since she'd arrived.

Cara turned and before he could step away, she lifted herself on her toes and brushed her lips against his cheek. The room spun and his skin burnt.

By the time he'd pulled himself together she was out of the room and he had to resist picking up the cushion a second time.

He didn't want Cara to leave in the morning, that wouldn't be right. He hardly knew Cara, and yet here she was staying in his house, learning all about his most secret business deals. He never trusted anyone this quickly.

If she was going to remain, then they had to establish some firmer ground rules for her stay.

To protect him from saying—or doing—something he'd regret.

If only he knew what those rules could be.

CHAPTER SIX

THE AIR WAS already warm by the time Cara woke the next morning. Late nights were common in Spain, but even after going to bed she'd ruminated for ages over the argument with Teo.

The sight of Teo screaming into the cushion had done something to her. It had been so unexpected, so revealing and so utterly unlike the Teo she knew. He was exposed, vulnerable. Losing his carefully constructed control. She didn't know whether to laugh or hug him.

It was possible…just a little possible that she hadn't handled the conversation about Pablo well. Teo's assumption that she wanted Pablo's money had been incredibly rude and each time she thought about it she became angry all over again. But he had apologised profusely. And said some very strange and personal things.

I don't know how to behave around you.

She understood that he was still sad about Pablo, but that still didn't explain why he was so strange around her. Did he think she was made of glass and would crack at the slightest touch? It was ridiculous. Yes, being back in Seville had brought back memories of Pablo, but not all of them were sad. She'd had a wonderful time reminiscing with Val about happy times last night and he didn't think the subject of Pablo was as fraught as Teo seemed to.

She missed Pablo, she still felt his loss in her bones. But she'd lived a third of her life since then. Now the loss of Pablo was wrapped up in her mind with the loss of her parents. Coming only three years after the death of her father, the two losses linked to her young adulthood. That made her the person she was.

People died. People left you. She wouldn't make the mistake of putting all her happiness on one person again, but that didn't mean she couldn't stand to say Pablo's name.

Despite Teo's promise that he would leave and stay in a hotel, she wondered if it might be best if she simply left to save them both another argument. She and Teo did not get along—she didn't much like him and for some reason or another he'd never liked her. It was clear to her now that they could never be friends.

Except…

There had been moments last night when they had been talking with his guests and looks had passed between them, small flashes of understanding. She knew what he was trying to say before he'd even said it. There had been times when the light had caught his eyes and they had warmed from black to a beautiful brown. When he'd smiled at her and her insides had turned inside out. Teo never smiled at her, yet he had at dinner.

And then there had been the buttons. Damn buttons. If she ever met the person who invented buttons that small she'd give them a piece of her mind. Teo had fumbled, and with each slip his fingers would brush against her bare neck, sending heat zipping down her spine.

What was that about? It was as though the air crackled around him. Like he produced his own electricity and she was a lightning rod.

Ridiculous. She was not attracted to Teo. Sure, he was good-looking, she could see that as well as anyone. And maybe she did find him attractive. But it wasn't the sort of feeling she could act on. That was simply out of the question. Besides, it wasn't as though he was interested in her. Far from it. So it wasn't attraction, but maybe appreciation. Entirely objective, of course.

Cara splashed water on her face, then ran her fingers through her hair. Movement was easier this morning somehow. Each day she felt noticeably better than the last. She'd only need to stay another day or so.

If she could handle being under the same roof as him, then Teo should be able to as well.

Cara opened the shutters and door but the courtyard was empty. The shutters on the other side were still closed as well. She walked back through her room and out to the entrance hall. Also quiet. Alba would no doubt be in the kitchen. She hoped Teo hadn't actually carried out his threat and left the house. His behaviour hadn't been perfect, but he didn't need to leave.

Yet there was no denying Teo was quite messed-up.

It's Pablo. *He loved Pablo, he misses him and having you here is more than he bargained for. Pablo is still a big part of Teo's life. More even than yours.*

Teo was brilliant, perhaps a little flawed, but who wasn't? Last night he had been charming, intelligent, great company. Everyone in the room had hung on every word he'd spoken. Val was engaging as well, but Teo was the one who held the room together.

There was noise in the kitchen. Alba would know if Teo had left, but it wasn't Alba standing at the coffee machine and swearing at it, it was Teo.

'Hey,' she said.

He spun. Teo looked stressed. For the first time since her arrival his hair wasn't brushed, but wild and sticking up in all directions. It suited him. If she had her way, he'd mess it up even more. She pressed her lips together and held back a smile.

A film of perspiration lay on his high forehead.

'What's up?'

'I can't get the coffee machine to work.'

'Where's Alba?'

He groaned. 'She's had to go away for a few days. Her daughter's unwell and she needs to help with her grandchildren.'

'Oh.'

'Geraldo's gone with her, so we're on our own.'

'Oh, well. If we needed a further sign that I should move to a hotel, this is it.'

He shook his head. 'No. I can manage.'

She raised an eyebrow. He did not look like a man who was managing.

'We're two grown-ups, surely we can look after ourselves for a day or two?' he said.

'Yet, you don't know how to make coffee.'

'I know how to make coffee. I just don't know how to work *this* machine. It's like you need a special degree for it.'

'Then use a pot.'

She opened a few cupboards and found a regular metal coffee-pot for brewing coffee on the stove. He stared at it.

'Do you know how to use this?' she asked.

'Of course.'

Then she laughed. 'Good, because I don't. I am utterly useless in a kitchen. I'm not sure I can even make toast.'

He stared at her. 'What?'

'I never learnt, I was never allowed to. Dad was determined that I wouldn't step into the role of housewife after my mother passed away, so he did the housework and cooking himself. Then I lived in halls at college and I've been on the road ever since.'

'But...'

'Look, can we just make a temporary truce? You won't criticise my way of life and I won't pick on you?'

'I wasn't going to criticise. Honestly. I'm the one who can't figure out his own coffee machine. I think since having Alba I've de-skilled somewhat.'

She could sympathise, not having developed many of the basic skills in the first place.

'Where do you keep your coffee grounds?'

He shrugged and she laughed again.

'Okay, this'll be fun.'

She went to the fridge, he went to the pantry. He produced an unopened pack of coffee, she produced an open one.

He took it from her with a smile.

'You should sit, I can do this,' he said.

'I'm fine.'

'Sit, please. Are you hungry?'

'If I say yes, will it be a problem?'

'Not at all, I can get us something.'

'Don't you have meetings today?'

'Not until later.'

Cara sat, partly because she was tired of arguing but mostly to see how Teo would manage getting her breakfast. He opened one cupboard after the next without finding what he was looking for. He wasn't even dressed, but wearing long pyjama pants and a white T-shirt. It took her one second to realise he wasn't wearing underwear under the pants, the thin fabric of which suggested a well-toned bottom. Her face warmed but she didn't look away.

Interesting.

Not simply the fact that Teo's butt was very watchable but also the fact that she wanted to watch. He was off guard and unguarded, with an especially firm bottom. She shouldn't think about what else was under that thin fabric, but she couldn't help herself.

Maybe what she felt was more than appreciation but a very unwelcome and awkward attraction. The realisation landed uncomfortably in her stomach.

No. She was hungry, that was all.

'I've never cooked in this kitchen. Alba made it her own.'

'I understand,' she said, getting a perverse pleasure in seeing Teo out of his depth. He always seemed together to the point of being uptight. Last night's argument the exception. She liked seeing Teo bemused. Flustered. Shaken.

She really was perverse.

Eventually Teo laid out a pot of fresh coffee, figs, peaches and strawberries, along with some bread and cheese on the large kitchen table, then sat with her. Cara sipped her coffee. It wasn't bad. Not as good as Alba's but she'd suffered through far worse.

'No wonder you couldn't find anything, this kitchen is enormous.'

Teo looked around as well as though he were also seeing it for the first time. The room had high ceilings like the rest of the house, marble bench tops, a big kitchen island. Like the rest of the house it had been renovated, though, she was glad to see, restored in a traditional style and not modernised into an impersonal default neutral. The walls were painted in pale blues and yellows and felt happy and calm all at once.

Teo could have ordered in some food, but he'd taken the time to make the breakfast himself and she was touched.

After he'd finished eating, Teo cleared his throat and said, with his serious face, 'I've been thinking. About your work. I know you've had to cancel your job here, and possibly others.'

She looked at her plate. 'Yes, I was due to be in Paris for a two-week job after this and I've had to find someone to take on that as well since I can't leave until after my check-up.'

'I understand.'

'I'm going to try to see if I can pick up some online work.'

He nodded. 'I also have an idea.'

Teo looked her straight in the eyes. His were not angry, but held a certain openness. Maybe even a spark of friendliness.

'It would be better for your health to stay in Seville for a few more weeks, until you're sure you've recovered.'

'What are you saying? That my business model is risky? My lifestyle unsustainable?'

'No, Cara, I wasn't going to say anything of the sort.'

'Though you think it.'

'I already told you, I don't think that at all. I don't have a problem with your way of life.'

No, but you have a problem with me. 'That's what you said, but…'

His brow creased with confusion. 'I really don't have an ulterior motive. You need a job for the next little while, but you need to stay in the vicinity of Seville. I'm suggesting you work for me.'

'Oh.'

'You can say no, but you were amazing last night. Doug and Jerry really liked you and you've established a rapport with them. If you could be available to help Val and I while we complete this deal, I would be grateful. You would be doing me a favour. And Val as well.'

She sat with the idea for a moment. Three days

ago, she would have dismissed the idea outright, but since starting to see another side of Teo, she wasn't as hasty. The idea did have some merit.

'They leave today, but will be back in about a week. If you're well enough by then—'

'I'll be well enough.'

'Then you'll do it?'

She'd walked into that one. She hoped to be well enough; the doctor had told her that after a week she might be fine to do light work if she felt up to it.

'Can I think about it?'

'Of course, and if you agree, I'll put you in touch with our contracts department. They will handle your pay and conditions and all those details. I won't need to be involved. While I would be happy to pay you anything you ask, I get the feeling you'd be more comfortable with the arrangement being made at arm's length from me.' His dark lips lifted into a soft smile. 'And, if you agree to stay, you will stay here. I owe it to Pablo to make sure you're okay.'

Far from being insensitive, if anything Teo was overly sensitive to everything surrounding her.

I don't know how to behave around you.

'Thank you, that's considerate. I will think about it.'

Teo stood. 'I'll be back at lunchtime to fix you something to eat.'

She laughed again. 'Teo, please, stay at the office. I'm not going to starve. Besides, Alba told me she'd left some soup in the fridge.'

His eye twitched. 'She did?'

He closed his eyes, breathed deeply and then exhaled, as though he was trying to calm himself.

But as though she could read his mind, she sensed what was wrong.

'Do you think Alba knew she wasn't going to be here?'

'I'm starting to think it might be a possibility.'

Though Cara couldn't think why Alba wouldn't tell them she may have to leave, by the way Teo was muttering under his breath he seemed to.

'Then I'll be back to prepare it for you.'

'You're working on a big deal, please just go.'

'And you won't leave?'

'Is that what you're worried about? That I'll sneak out?'

He didn't answer.

'I promise I won't leave.'

She couldn't leave now. Apart from anything, someone needed to look after him. Teo was nearly as hopeless in a kitchen as she was, which was saying something. Besides, watching him fumble around, trying to make her breakfast when he clearly didn't know what he was doing was… sweet. Yes, strangely sweet.

Teo was not the impenetrable force she'd always thought. Something about his vulnerability made her heart warm a little more to him.

He was offering her a way through her financial problems. This way there was a chance she might be able to gather enough money to engage the lawyers to fight for her house after all. She closed her eyes and drew in a deep breath. Her parents' house, with its wind-battered shingles and the flowering dogwood in the front yard.

But it wasn't just that.

Besides, Pablo had loved Teo.

She could at least try to like him as well.

Alba. She'd get a piece of his mind when she returned.

Are you going to demand evidence of her daughter's health? If Alba needed some time off, she just could have asked. Granted, it wasn't ideal timing given Cara was staying but he wouldn't have refused.

Now he came to think of it, there was a larger number of prepared meals in the fridge than usual. Alba had planned to leave, Teo was certain. Though he was less certain if Alba's reasons for leaving were as noble as she claimed.

Misguided matchmaking.

He ground his teeth together as he showered and dressed. Alba was barking up the wrong tree, so to speak. She'd put two and two together and ended up with ten. Pick your favourite idiom, Alba was wrong. He and Cara could barely have a conversation without arguing. They'd never be anything more than acquaintances, and now, temporary colleagues. Alba had been so excited by the idea of a woman coming to stay with them she'd jumped to all the wrong conclusions.

He should have predicted it. Of late her hints that it was time for him to find a girlfriend had gone from subtle to outright blatant. He forgave her because he knew she meant well, but this time?

This time he wasn't sure what he'd say to her. Cara wasn't just any other woman, and what he felt about her was far too complicated to be able to humour Alba and her machinations.

Teo went into the office, attended the meetings he had to in person and in the middle of the day came home, via the *panadería*, with some bread and cake.

The house was quiet when he returned, the shutters to Cara's room closed. He left the bread and a spread of food from the fridge out on the bench in the kitchen and went to his study.

The deal with the producers was in its early stages. Doug and Jerry were interested but there were so many other things to consider than just money. Things like who would write the script, what their vision for the film was. How much of a say Teo and Val would have in the production. How they intended to represent Pablo's game.

There was a knock at his open office door and he turned. Even though he knew it would be Cara, he was still not prepared. Not for the sight of her, certainly not for the way she walked confidently in, hips swinging and her riotous hair falling down around her shoulders. She was wearing the same thin pyjamas but now looked brighter somehow. There was more colour in her cheeks each time he saw her. A lump moved from his throat, swallowed into his chest and down into his gut. He couldn't even find the breath to say *Hello.*

'I've been thinking about your offer.'

And? Offering her work had seemed like the decent thing to do since he'd messed up the night before and wanted to make it up to her. And he hadn't lied when he'd told her that she would be an asset to him and Val; the producers had warmed to her and even though he and Val spoke conversational English, when it came to negotiating the terms of a detailed contract, it was far easier with an interpreter assisting.

He wasn't sure how he was going to feel about her answer either way.

'And I'd like to accept.'

'Great, I'm glad,' he said, but his body had grown tight.

It was the right thing to do, and yet, he didn't feel like himself when Cara was around and he wasn't sure how he was going to manage that over the next few weeks. Along with everything else. His body seemed to react to Cara's presence before his brain had a chance to engage, requiring him to constantly remind himself who she was and why these feelings were wrong. It was the last thing he needed right now.

'I'll let our contracts department know and they can get something drawn up for you.'

She nodded, stepped away from his desk, and he could see the moment she first focused on her surroundings. His office.

Her eyes first travelled behind him to the floor-to-ceiling glass doors that opened down onto the courtyard, then to her left into the wall of bookcases, holding books, awards, photographs. Then they moved across his desk to the many computer monitors and finally to the wall with a display of framed prints. She walked over to them, and he kicked himself for not showing her out once their business had concluded.

'These are...' Cara lifted an index finger to one, but didn't touch the print. She walked to the next and stared at it even closer. There was no point fibbing. It was immediately apparent to anyone who knew him. These were the sketches upon which their first game, *Matador*, had been based.

'Yes, they're Pablo's,' he said. His tongue suddenly too big for his mouth. She turned to him, eyes wide and glassy but he could see the thoughts ticking over.

'Of course,' she whispered and kept staring.

'They remind me of him,' he said, for no reason at all. Teo's voice cracked on 'him.'

She nodded. 'I know he was important to you.'

'Very. Without Pablo I wouldn't be here today. I owe him a great debt. I owe him everything.'

Cara continued to slowly study the prints, moving from one to the next. After a while, once his gut was well and truly tangled in tight knots, she turned. 'He's still at the centre of your world, isn't he?'

'I don't… I mean, maybe. Yes.' He didn't know what she was getting at.

'Isn't that hard? Don't you feel that it's holding you back?'

'I don't know what you mean, and no, of course it isn't hard. It's an honour to be able to develop and sell Pablo's creations.'

Cara studied him through narrowed, focused eyes, looking at him so closely she could probably see that his heart was pounding to get out of his ribcage.

'Why don't you like me? What did I do?' she asked.

He shook his head.

'I'm serious, don't dismiss me. If I'm going to work for you then I need to know what I'm doing that has offended you so much.'

'I've told you, nothing.'

'Then why did you never speak to me?'

Pablo had been so happy, so in love. Teo envied his ability to fall for someone—anyone—so early, so naturally. Teo had never been able to.

He found it hard enough to open up to anyone, let alone take a plunge like falling in love. In love. He wasn't even sure what that felt like. He couldn't imagine trusting someone to take that kind of plunge. It would be like diving into a pool with no idea how deep it was. Far too dangerous.

'Because I'm me.'

'Is that supposed to be a reason?' She didn't laugh, for which he was grateful, but she stood, steadfast, waiting for him to say more. Him feeling like she was taking a knife to his chest and peeling his skin away. Just by looking at him.

'I have a hard time talking to new people.' He didn't trust people easily, and he couldn't trust Cara.

No. You can't trust yourself.

He'd known that since the first day they had met, when Pablo had introduced them and she'd smiled and his first and only thought had been—*Damn.*

Because he could see so well, so clearly how Pablo could fall head over heels for this woman. Teo had stopped himself doing the very same thing just in time.

Cara and Pablo were together.

He and Cara could never be.

'Spare me the Mr Darcy line.'

'It's not a line.'

Truly. Teo had always been a happy child, but everything that had happened with his father had taught him a valuable lesson: *Don't trust anyone. Nothing is as it seems.*

'Can I make you dinner this evening? As a kind of apology?'

'You think cooking for me is a good way to apologise? Sounds like you want to hurt me even more.'

It took him a beat to realise she was kidding. Her face opened into a smile and he let his follow.

Cara sat and made a point of watching him as he fumbled around the kitchen. He wasn't sure where everything was and opened each cupboard more than once to locate things. He was serving bread, cheese and some of the leftovers from the night before. It shouldn't have been this hard. But it was. And having Cara sit at the bench and watch him was not helping one bit.

'If you're looking for the plates, they're in that cupboard on the left.' She pointed.

He had been looking for the plates and she was right. He'd opened this cupboard not two minutes ago when he was trying to find the glasses.

It wasn't as though he didn't know his own kitchen at all, but having an audience, and an audience who was watching him as intently as Cara, was off-putting.

He should've felt better now she'd agreed to stay and work with him. Except now she was asking questions about why he didn't like her, why he'd always been so distant around her. His answers were pathetic—at best. He was a grown-up, a successful businessman, he should know how to behave around a woman. Even a woman he found as beguiling as Cara.

Maybe it was a good thing he didn't feel like himself when she was around. He felt uncertain, but also full of anticipation. He felt untethered, but also a sense of lightness.

'Did it not occur to you that you could've ordered something in?' she asked.

He closed his eyes as he remembered that restaurants and delivery people existed.

'This is much better for you,' he said.

'Perhaps. The pre-show is pretty entertaining.'

He ignored the insult. Their truce was too fresh.

'I'm trying to look after you and I promised you a housekeeper.'

'Things have changed. You don't have to do everything yourself.'

'I do though.'

'Why?'

'It's the way I am.' There was food here, healthy food, they didn't need to go out. Besides, he'd given her his word that he'd look after her. He wouldn't go back on that.

'But why?' she asked.

'Because it's the right thing to do. You understand that, don't you?'

She shook her head. 'I like to do things properly, I take care to get things right, but I forgive myself for not getting everything right. I'm human. And so are you.'

He shook his head again. It was so easy for some people. Other people. People whose father had not swindled others out of millions of euros. People who didn't have to constantly prove to the world that they were worthy of trust.

Other people.

Not him.

After they ate—a meal not as good as one of Alba's but not a bad effort—Cara tried to help him clean up but he was adamant she sit.

'I've been sitting all day. And lying down. I need to move around.'

'I'm sure packing a dishwasher is not what Dr Magdalena had in mind.'

'I'd love to go for a walk.'

He drew a breath but she waved him down. 'Not a long one. Just around the block. It's allowed,' she said.

'I'll come with you.'

'You don't have to.'

'And if I want to?'

He wasn't going to force his company on her but he'd feel much better if someone was with her. She looked brighter and seemed well but only five days ago she'd been on an operating table. Cara nodded and he exhaled.

Outside, the sun was just setting and the streetlights were coming on. The city wouldn't really start to come alive again until it was dark, when the streets, the cafés and bars would be buzzing with conversation, laughter and music. Right now, though, the air was humid but cooling. Cara walked slowly and he kept pace beside her.

'Where do your family live?' she asked.

'My family?'

'Yes, you know all about mine, I'm curious about yours. If we're going to be friends.'

Friends? Colleagues and acquaintances was fine. But friends? Friends was something different. But any more resistance would only lead to more questioning.

Besides, he didn't know all about Cara's family, only the outline. Only that she had no family or no family able or willing to come to her hospital bed in Seville. But not knowing things about Cara made everything else easier. Because the more he found out about her, the more he thought about her, and the more he thought about her… well…the more he wanted to know and the cycle began again.

'I have three younger siblings. They all live around here.'

'Santa Cruz?'

'No, but in Seville.'

'And your parents?'

She was circling the topic like a shark. She wasn't going to swim away until he gave her something. Her motives were not malicious; she was genuinely curious. For most people the question 'Tell me about your parents?' was benign.

But not for Teo.

This is Cara, you can trust her. Pablo did.

Hadn't Pablo told her about his father? No, he doubted it. Pablo knew how fiercely Teo protected his privacy. Pablo would've known that this was Teo's business and no one else's. And if Cara did know about his father, then she probably wouldn't be asking these questions. Teo looked out over the square and took a deep breath.

'When I was twelve, my father was charged with multiple counts of investment fraud. His case went to trial and it was very big news at the time because he cheated so many people out of so much money. He was eventually convicted and sent to prison. He died there six years ago now.'

Cara sucked in a deep breath. He didn't look at her, it was easier that way.

'I'm so sorry, I had no idea.'

'I don't talk about it and those close to me know that. I'm not surprised Pablo didn't tell you.'

Although part of him *was* surprised because he somehow assumed that Pablo had told Cara everything, though he wasn't sure why.

'I thought we had money, but it turns out everything we owned belonged to other people. We moved out of the house I grew up in and my mother moved me, my brother and my sisters into a rented apartment. She went back to work and supported us.'

'That's awful. Did she…'

'Did she know what he'd been doing?'

Cara nodded.

'No, she trusted my father and believed his business was legitimate, but then so many people did.'

He let her sit with that information for a while and waited for her to step further away from him, half expected her to make an excuse and leave his house. He wasn't anticipating her next words. 'There's nothing worse than trusting someone and having them let you down, is there?'

He shook his head. He couldn't think of anything at all.

'Thank you for telling me, Teo. I understand a little better now.'

She meant that as a good thing, but Teo only felt more exposed. Cara placed her hand on his upper arm, her hand small, her touch light, yet his entire body was entirely under her control. He wanted to pull her to him, to hold her, fall into her touch. But that was impossible. Yet stepping back from her touch was too. The corners of her gorgeous pink mouth lifted into a smile and her eyes looked at him as if anticipating an answer.

He wanted to return her smile, answer the question she was asking, but he was too shaken by the intensity of the situation, of everything he'd just told her. He'd already revealed too much of himself to her and he had to stop there. Cara dropped her hand and stepped away.

When Teo finally focused back on his surroundings he saw they were back at his front door.

'I'm exhausted, I'm going to turn in, if that's okay,' she said.

He couldn't argue. They had only walked a single lap of the small square and he felt as though he'd run a marathon.

CHAPTER SEVEN

THEY FOLLOWED A similar pattern for the next few days. At breakfast, Cara would point to the cupboards, direct him where things belonged, while Teo prepared the meal and cleaned up again.

Together they found a nearby grocery store, and decided what to order and organised delivery. Teo would go to the office, returning in the afternoon to work at home. Cara rested, read when she had the energy, watched television when she didn't.

They would eat dinner together and then go for a walk around the square. Each evening, as she regained her strength, their walks became longer. Slow walks encouraged slow, thoughtful conversations. As the walks became longer, they fell into the habit of finding a bench partway through and watching the world go by. The people going to bars, those coming home again.

Cara told him about her home in Woods Hole, her childhood, idyllic, until her mother died. She didn't dwell on the loss of her parents at the ages of ten and seventeen, instead talked more about the last decade of her life, her life on the road. One evening, as they were sitting on the bench she had come to think of as theirs, Teo surprised her by saying, 'Despite what you might think I do envy you the freedom of your lifestyle.'

Where had that come from? Even after nearly a week of living under the same roof, the workings of Teo's mind were still a mystery to her.

'Freedom?' she asked.

'You're not tied down anywhere. You go where you choose and when you choose. It must be kind of nice.'

'It's not all freedom. I can't do anything I want. I have to make a living. And it's not always easy. Sometimes I have a lot of work, sometimes I don't have enough.' And sometimes she got sick and couldn't work.

But she did feel a certain lightness, there was comfort in knowing that she'd never become so attached to something or someone that she could be hurt again. That was the true freedom. Yet, the pull Seville had over her was strange. Leaving this beautiful pink house would be hard.

'I know about your parents but what about siblings? Grandparents?' he asked.

'My grandparents are all gone, my father was older than my mother and I never knew his parents. My mother didn't have a great relationship with hers but they're gone now as well.'

'No siblings?'

Teo had told her all about his brother and sisters, four kids in one family was such a foreign concept to Cara, who may as well have been an only child.

'I have a half-brother, my father's son from a previous relationship, but we're not close.'

'Why not?'

'That's a long story, maybe one for another time.'

'You don't have time now?'

He was going to get the answer out of her eventually so she might as well tell him.

'His name is Liam. He's ten years older than I am. Even though he stayed with my dad, our father, pretty regularly, it was always better when he wasn't there.'

'Any particular reason?'

She shrugged. 'I think he resented my mother. And maybe me. I don't really know.'

When she was younger it had bothered her that Liam didn't like her, she'd craved the attention and affection of her older sibling but had never received it. She'd spent more time than she cared to admit wondering what she had done until she'd realised that whatever the reason was it was his business and his problem.

'When Dad died, it was awful. Liam was executor of his estate.'

'I have a horrible feeling where this is going.'

'Yeah, well, my father had a will, and it made Liam not just the executor but my guardian. As executor, Liam managed to get the house transferred into his name, with some money put in trust for me until I turned twenty-five.'

'And?'

'When I turned twenty-five, I found out the account was mostly empty. He argued that he'd used the money to support me, which wasn't true at all. My college tuition was paid out of the money, but otherwise I had to work to support myself. What was left was not even enough to engage lawyers to fight it.'

'Oh, Cara, I'm so sorry.' Teo bunched his fists. He was struggling to contain something inside him.

'I've been trying to get lawyers to fight it ever since. But given the complexities of the case they want a down payment before they take it on. Even if I did get a judgement in my favour, we don't know what he did with the money.'

'He gave you nothing?' Teo's face was red in the evening sun.

'Just my tuition, as I said. And anytime I asked for more he'd tell me how generous he'd been. How I needed to be more careful with money.'

Teo bit his lip.

He's angry.

Cara had been angry too. Once upon a time.

Until she realised it wasn't helping her get on with her life.

'Your parents' house? Did you fight for it?'

'I'm going to try. But it's in his name, he lives there with his wife and children. The lawyers have told me not to get my hopes up.'

'That's outrageous.'

She was touched by Teo's anger, but at the same time, it was an anger that she had to try hard to keep under control herself. It was complicated.

'Yes and no. I don't like the idea of kicking my niece and nephew out of their home.'

'But it was your home too.'

She sighed. It was all she could do. There was no happy ending for everyone in this story.

'You deserve something.'

Again, she sighed. She wanted Liam to suffer, but she didn't want to hurt anyone else. She simply wanted her rightful share. A nest egg. Something to fall back on when she could no longer travel the world.

'One thing I want is my mother's jewellery. A few gold necklaces. A pearl ring. Some antique brooches.'

'And he won't give you those?'

She shook her head.

'But it isn't his property.'

She laughed. 'Try telling that to him and his wife. She had the nerve to wear the ring the last time I saw them.'

'When was that?'

'A few years ago, now. When I was still trying to maintain a relationship with his children.'

But no longer. It was too painful, too complicated.

'I see now,' Teo said.

'What?'

'Why you don't stay in one place.'

'I don't know where I would stay. I don't feel at home anywhere, or rather, I don't feel any special connection to any one place.' *Apart from my old home*. 'I wouldn't know where to choose.' She gave a nervous laugh. She'd just admitted something deeply personal to someone she wasn't even sure she could trust.

'Since we're sharing, I have a few questions for you. Why do you work so hard? What's it all for? You don't seem to have a partner. A family of your own. You work ridiculous hours, but for what? As far as I can tell, the thing that you care about the most is Pablo's charity.'

'That's not true,' he said.

She looked at him but didn't have to speak. Her raised eyebrow said everything she wanted to.

'The charity is important, I can't see how you could possibly find fault with that.'

She softened. 'Not a fault. I'm just wondering when you get a turn.'

'A turn at what?'

She laughed. 'Exactly, you're too busy putting

everyone and everything else first you don't even realise you're a person too.'

'I do,' he said but confusion creased his face.

His father. He would have cast a dark shadow over Teo's childhood.

She didn't hate Teo. And she was beginning to wonder if he didn't really hate her.

Teo stood. It had become dark while they had been sitting on their bench. Cara braced herself to stand, still tender from the surgery, but before she stood Teo offered her his hand. She took it and she felt weightless as she rose. Her head spun.

'Thank you.' Her voice was far softer than she meant it to be. She didn't drop his hand immediately and nor did he. Teo looked down at her, a shadow of a smile on his lips, his eyes no longer shuttered, but open and welcoming. She felt herself falling closer to him, wanting to feel more than just his hand, but his arms, his chest. All of him.

He let go of her and she had to stop herself from grabbing his hand again. She wanted the warmth, the sense of safety. She wanted to feel that hand on her arm, on her shoulder, on her back. Everywhere.

No. No. She mustn't confuse this new friendship with anything else. She was glad she and Teo had become friends, but these absurd longings she was having about Teo had to stop.

* * *

Two weeks after Cara's surgery, Alba was still away, looking after her daughter, whose illness seemed to be dragging on for quite a long time. Anytime Cara ventured to ask about Alba, Teo got annoyed, so she left the topic alone.

Far from being a prison sentence, her stay with Teo had flown by. It helped that Teo was starting to get her involved in the work as well; she'd sat in on a few video conferences with the producers and investors and before she knew it, she was due for her check-up with Dr Magdalena.

Teo offered to drive her but she knew he was due at the office at that time.

'I can catch a cab.'

'I'll get you a driver.'

She laughed, 'I am well.'

Teo sighed and disappeared into his office.

He returned moments later and held out his hand to her. 'Here.'

It was a key. Cara opened her hand and he dropped the silver key into her palm.

'What's this?'

'A key to the house. You'll need it to get back in when I'm at work. I'm sorry, I should have thought about giving you one earlier.'

She shook her head and turned the key over and over in her hand. A key to the pink house. She couldn't remember the last time she'd held a key to something that wasn't a hotel room or short-term apartment.

No. She could.

The key to her house in Woods Hole. She'd tried to use it the last time she visited Liam, only to find that it no longer fit. Liam and Avril had changed the locks. She winced at the memory, then pushed it aside.

The doctor was happy with Cara's progress but told her to listen to her body. 'You can do anything. I mean, I wouldn't lift anything too heavy, but working, driving, stairs, exercise are all okay.'

'What sort of exercise?' She didn't want to have to stop her evening walks with Teo. They were one of the highlights of her day.

'Walking, running. Sex.'

'That wasn't what I meant… I haven't…' Cara gulped and Dr Magdalena smiled.

You haven't thought about that? Of course you've been thinking about it. You've been imagining Teo and what it would be like to make love to him. It's some sort of perverse want-what-you-can't-have thing because there's no way he'd want to sleep with you.

Although, her relationship with Teo *was* changing. They were getting closer, in a two-steps-forward, one-step-back dance. She'd catch him looking at her and he'd be smiling, but as soon as he realised he'd been caught, the shutters would go up again.

Or they'd be easily talking away about anything and everything under the sun and then he'd clam up. Make an excuse to leave.

Teo had been wrong, he did know how to behave around her, only not all of the time.

As she made her way back from the doctor's to the pink house, she wondered if that was really what she wanted. She would miss him when she left. She'd become used to being under the same roof with someone, comfortable living with him, happy spending time with him. Someone who knew how she liked her coffee in the morning.

Yet. It was all temporary.

Live in the moment.

It was advice she often had to give herself. *Live in the moment. You can't revisit the past and the future isn't yet written.*

After she was cleared by Dr Magdalena, Cara joined Teo with the work in earnest. She sat in on the negotiations with the producers, Val and Teo, and otherwise stayed not far from Teo's side, reminding him what had been said, mulling over ideas. Much of her usual work consisted of interpreting in detailed business negotiations, so it wasn't just Spanish and English she was proficient at. She often surprised herself how much legal and business knowledge she actually had.

For the first few days everything went well, but negotiations became tense when they began discussing the prospect of sequels. Doug and Jerry had some ideas that did not match Val and Teo's wishes.

There was a lot of goodwill between the parties, but Teo must have sensed that they were in danger of the deal breaking down.

One afternoon in Teo's office at home, he said, 'I think we need another circuit breaker. Another social occasion, something informal,' he said.

'Another dinner? With me as well?' Cara asked.

'Of course, if you're amenable.'

'Why wouldn't I be?' This was her job now, he was paying her.

'Val thinks we should take them for a flamenco evening.' He sounded hesitant.

'I love flamenco. I've always wanted to learn.'

'Well, it could just be your lucky day.'

Cara was familiar with the sort of thing they had in mind, an evening of drinks and tapas, while they watched a performance, followed by a lesson and then more dancing with everyone. A quintessential Sevillian experience.

'You can think of something better?' she asked.

'No, that's the thing.' He frowned and she laughed.

'It's a great idea. Why the long face? You think it's too touristy? Too cliché?'

'No.'

'Then what?'

Teo looked at her, deeply. So intently she felt exposed.

'Me?' Teo the grump strikes again. Did he not want to go dancing with her?

He shrugged. 'In case you're not well enough.'

His concern was strange. And unnecessary.

'I'll be fine. And I'll take it easy, I promise.'

Teo frowned again. Would she ever figure him out?

Teo's assistant arranged it all. A night of flamenco, tapas and music.

Teo went into his office to do some other work. After reading her emails, referring some work to other interpreters, she was at a loose end.

In preparation for the evening, Cara flicked through her clothes, which were now hung neatly in her wardrobe. She didn't have anything that was exactly right for a flamenco lesson. Her dresses were either too businesslike or too casual.

It was another beautiful day, bright, but not too warm, with a gentle breeze. She liked that she was able to get out and about and move again. Apart from the occasional twinge she felt as good as she had a month ago. She caught a cab to Calle Sierpes, a pedestrianised street in the heart of Seville. She wandered along the bustling street and associated laneways.

She'd been here only once before, with Pablo, but hadn't lingered long at the fashion stores. He'd been impatient to show her some nearby art galleries and she'd never come back.

Even though she didn't collect many things, Cara still loved wandering around the shopping districts and markets of each town she visited, seeing what was unique and what seemed to stay the same no matter what country she was in. She loved watching the people going busily about their days and the ones sitting at cafés, meeting people. All the activities of everyday life. She also loved clothes. Even though she didn't own many, she liked to choose each piece with care and with longevity in mind. Today was no different. Even though she knew she may not have much use for this dress beyond her stay in Seville, she enjoyed wandering from store to store looking at the clothes. In a boutique in a laneway off the main street she tried on several dresses, each lovelier than the last.

In the end it came down to two dresses: a dark green one that felt safe and conservative, and a bright red one that would ensure she stood out. The red dress had a full skirt, not as decadent or frilly as a traditional flamenco dress, but it would be something that would swish around her legs, in the way she'd always admired. It was beautiful, but what if she wasn't in the mood to stand out?

'The second one is half price. You should get both,' the sales assistant said, and at that moment Cara had no good argument against it. So she did.

* * *

Cara met the men, who had come directly from the office, at the restaurant. Four pairs of eyes turned to her when she entered and the air cracked with tension, but they smiled as one when they saw her. All except Teo, whose smile almost immediately turned down into a frown when their eyes met.

Cara's heart dropped and her eyes cast down at her outfit. She'd worked up the courage to wear the red dress and didn't know what was wrong. She thought she looked good, but Teo's reaction suggested otherwise.

Val slid up to her. 'Wow, you look beautiful.'

Cara's gaze flicked past Val to Teo, whose eyes now looked thunderous.

'Don't worry about him, it's been a tense afternoon. We're counting on you to save this deal,' Val said.

'Me?' she spluttered.

Val laughed, 'I'm kidding, but we do need a break from money talk. If the deal falls through it will be because Doug is too tight and Teo is too stubborn. You know how he is when it comes to Pablo.'

'Touchy? Illogical?'

'And then some.'

'Why is he like that?' she asked.

'You tell me.' Val shrugged.

'I don't know, I hardly know him. You're his best friend.'

'He thinks he owes Pablo a huge debt. One he can never possibly repay. Most of it is in his head.'

This was as much as Cara herself had surmised over the past few weeks, Teo thought that he owed most of his success to Pablo and the game he created. As brilliant as Pablo had been and as much as she'd loved him, Cara knew that Verdadero's success was as much due to the grit and energy Teo had invested in the business as Pablo's contribution.

'But why? You and Teo have been responsible for Verdadero over the past ten years.'

'It isn't just the business. Pablo was his friend when no one else was. And now, well, I think he feels conflicted.'

'Conflicted? Why? Because of the movie deal?'

Val shook his head. 'No. Not that.'

She couldn't ask Val to explain because the sound of clapping hands signalled the beginning of the evening.

Their instructors were Santiago and Luiza and they began the evening by performing the flamenco with one another. Drinks were served, and the small crowd began to relax before Luiza said, 'Okay, now it's time for you all to try.'

Doug caught Cara's eye but then he looked behind her and slipped away.

Cara turned her head. Teo was on his feet, holding his hand out to her.

'Wonderful! You make a lovely couple. And there are plenty of women here for you, gentleman,' Luiza said.

Luiza lead Doug away to find another partner and Cara and Teo faced one another.

'Will you be okay?' Teo asked, his face no longer stormy but soft with concern.

'I'm fine, Teo, really.' She slipped her hand into his and there was that familiar electricity again. Why did his body feel different to other people's? Her body would recognise his touch blindfolded. The heat alone would give him away.

The couples were directed to drop hands and stand two feet from one another. Fortunately, the dance involved very few instances when the couples had to touch, but consisted mostly of complicated steps and hand movements, so there was little opportunity for further sparks to crackle between them.

Teo, as a native Sevillian, was naturally familiar with the movements. Val, who had at one point considered being a professional dancer, was proficient. Cara had to listen carefully to the instructions.

'You will learn the Sevillanas, Seville's own flamenco. It is about passion, sadness. Fire, darkness.' Santiago spoke forcefully. 'But also, elegance, strength. Intensity.'

Cara wasn't sure how she could possibly be all those things at once. While remembering all the steps.

Santiago explained the footwork, stomps, heel strikes, pointing of the toes. Luiza then followed by demonstrating the *braceo* and the *floreo*—the circular movement of the torso and the way to move the hands, wrists and fingers in circular motions.

They went through the steps so quickly Cara couldn't keep up.

'Can you repeat that please?' Cara asked but Santiago shook his head.

'Don't worry so much about the steps. You must use your body to show your emotions.'

'But I don't know what to do,' she said.

'Show your emotions! Show your passion!'

Cara sighed. If only it were that easy. If only passion was something she could share with the people in this room. With her dance partner, Teo.

Teo stepped towards her and whispered, 'The flamenco is as much about improvisation as the steps. Don't worry. Let the music and the beat inspire you.'

Cara closed her eyes, focused on the guitar and the doleful singing of the *cantor* and did as she was told, relaxed into the music. Her body found the beat.

She lifted her arms as she had seen Luiza do, stood tall, trying to appear more confident than she felt, and turned her body from the hips as Luiza was doing.

Teo stomped his feet, Cara followed his lead, though not his movements, the movements for men and women were subtly different. Once they were both moving, she tried to worry less about whether the movements were technically correct. No one else was watching her, they were all too focused on their own dance. The only person watching her was Teo.

She followed Teo, but also made things up, rolled her hands in the *floreo* movement, mixed the steps she remembered from Santiago and Luiza's quick lesson together.

But she didn't relax. She and Teo reflected one another's moves. They didn't touch one another, but the sustained eye contact they were required to hold with one another was enough to make her heart pound. Teo's expression was no longer annoyed, but unfamiliar. His lids slightly lowered, he looked almost drowsy, yet his body was anything but. Lithe, flexible. Strong. Cara was almost too breathless to move and slowed her pace to almost a standstill. But once she did, Teo began to move around her in a circle, stomping his feet, and she had to watch him up close. The line of perspiration across his forehead, the concentration on his face. The flash of light in his eyes when he looked down at her. She could feel his steps through the floorboards and they made her knees weak.

'Relax, *señora*,' Luiza said as she passed. 'Don't worry about the steps, just surrender to the passion.'

Teo was getting closer and closer to her. The air around her shifted with his movements, his attention entirely focused on her. Single-minded. She felt as if she might melt. Would he get so close that he touched her, and where would he touch her if he did? Her hand? Her arm? Her cheek? Or would he press his hip against hers? Which did she want more? These were the thoughts filling Cara's mind when she should have been learning where to put her arms and when to stomp her feet. She had to start moving too, she couldn't just stand there. She lifted her leg and brought her shoe down hard. She expected to feel floorboards but instead felt something solid. Warm. And alive. Teo. He winced but said nothing.

'Oh, Teo, I'm sorry, I…'

'It's fine. I'm wearing boots.'

'We don't have to do this, you know?'

'I know, but you want to learn, don't you?'

She did. She'd always imagined doing this dance. And he knew it. Since she'd stupidly announced her ambition earlier that day.

'Then we'll learn. Let's focus.' He dragged his index finger along her jaw-line, dictating the direction her gaze should take, directly to his eyes.

He might as well have scorched her. The sparks travelled from his fingertip, over her skin, down her neck and straight to her core. Like two magnets, they held each other's eyes for a long moment, heavy, caught. *Frozen* wasn't the right word, since it felt as though steam was coming off both their bodies.

'Perfect,' murmured a voice. Santiago's. 'Now, use your hands.'

This was their cue to lift their hands to the sides of one another's faces. Not touching, just framing each other and not losing eye contact.

Her stomach, insides, everything had flipped over so many times she wasn't sure she'd ever be able to gather it all up and walk away. When Dr Magdalena had given clearance for physical activity, she doubted she'd had this in mind. Being totally and utterly consumed doing the flamenco with a very handsome man. Not to mention hot, hard and literally smouldering. A walk around the square was one thing. Heck, even sex with most of the men she'd been with hadn't left her this breathless. The air was warm and the smell of her perfume and Teo's aftershave wrapped around them both.

She could hardly breathe. Teo, she now saw, was holding his breath as well.

That's why he's so tense. He feels the same awkwardness as you.

His brown eyes appeared black in the half-light, and half hidden by his lids. He was a ridiculously handsome man. She'd known this, in theory. But this dance, this position they were now in was no longer theoretical. His arm was around her. He was holding her body closely, protectively against the side of his, looking down at her, his hand hovered next to her face and his eyes watching her. Not just watching her but *seeing* her.

Oh my.

No wonder this dance was so famous. It wasn't the clapping or guitar or the castanets. It was this. This look. Holding one another's gazes in an unbroken grip. It was intimate, vulnerable. You couldn't do this dance properly without getting a glimpse into your partner's soul.

And that's what she glimpsed now. Even as she sensed him moving her, leading her gently for the next few steps, she was unaware of her feet, practically floating. All she was aware of was his heartbeat. Thumping in time with hers. Forget the stomping or the clapping, as loud as it was, all she felt was his heart.

He, in turn, was showing her his soul. She'd never seen this look in his eyes before, so exposed, so vulnerable. Like she could read his emotions. It was like Santiago had said—passion. Fire. And most of all, intensity.

How could he act like he disliked her and yet look at her like this? She felt herself melting, clinging to him to stay upright. But the harder she held on to him, the stronger he held her.

He's not going to let you fall. He's not going to let you down.

Yet what was his deal? Obviously, he had a saviour complex, he was determined to help those in need. And did that include her? Was she just one of his projects? He was looking after her to repay the debt he thought he owed to Pablo. Maybe, maybe that was it.

From somewhere she heard Luiza's voice. 'Remember the Sevillanas is special. You may improvise. You are telling each other a story.'

'A story?' Cara whispered.

'We all tell ourselves stories. Some of them are true, and some of them are just in our head,' Teo replied.

He was right. She told herself all kinds of stories. How her parents had really loved her, how they would be horrified to know what Liam had done. How what had happened to Pablo wasn't her fault. She didn't always believe these stories.

'What stories do you tell yourself?' she whispered.

He was silent for so long she thought he was ignoring her question but then he said, 'That I must do everything right, that I'm being judged. I owe my success to Pablo and I don't know how I can ever repay him.'

He'd never been so honest with her and her

heart went out to him. *No*, she wanted to say, *it isn't. You don't owe Pablo anything. People care for you, no matter what*, but her mouth was too dry. Teo was standing close to her, his scent wrapping its way through her body and her thoughts. It was too much and she closed her eyes.

She realised with surprise that she already knew Teo's story, that he had to fix everything and everyone. That his worst nightmare would be doing something wrong. Being like his father. Her heart cracked a little for the boy finding out that his father was not the person he thought he was, for the man now holding her in his arms who was too scared to live his authentic life in case he made some sort of mistake. She wanted to slide her hand up his arm, to cradle his face in her palm and tell him that everything would be okay, that he was not his father. That he had proven himself to be a good man many times over.

'What story do you tell yourself?' he asked.

Without opening her eyes she whispered, 'That everyone I love leaves, that the only person I can depend on is myself.'

Oh. The honesty of those words made her eyes pop open. She'd never admitted that to herself, much less to anyone else. The only thing she saw were Teo's brown eyes, looking back at her. The rest of the cantina had disappeared.

Brown and unguarded for once, they reflected her own back at her. His eyes were wide with a question, but a question she couldn't identify, much less answer.

The click of fingers near her face brought them both back to the present.

'*Señora*, I can see you are keen to get to the part where you declare your love, but first you have to learn the steps. It is not just love, but struggle and intensity and first must come darkness.'

Cara's face burnt at the suggestion she might declare her love to anyone, let alone Teo.

Love! That was ridiculous. What she felt for Teo was attraction and confusion. Love had nothing to do with it.

From the moment Cara arrived at the cantina things started going wrong. Or right. Teo wasn't sure. She wore a dress of flaming flamenco red, with a long full skirt and a neckline that scooped down low to the swell of her breasts. Breasts he'd been trying to believe were not as beautiful as he'd imagined but now could no longer deny. Her hair was half up, fastened with a clip and showing her face and smile but also flowing around her shoulders. His decision to offer to dance with Cara had been instinctual, rather than fully thought out, for which he'd suffered the consequences.

There had been moments, though, as they had danced, when he'd forgotten that he wasn't meant to be enjoying himself and had surrendered himself to it. Surrendered himself to the music. And to Cara.

And nothing bad had happened. Neither of them had exploded or cracked, even though there had been times when he'd felt he might self-combust.

It was the most erotic moment in his life and they had both been fully clothed. Only their gazes were connecting. Holding one another's. Not letting go.

Cara was Pablo's girlfriend and off-limits. And it wasn't just that. Cara was a free spirit; she made the entire world her home. Even if she did settle anywhere, what was to say she would choose Seville? No. Letting himself get close to her would only bring trouble that he couldn't afford.

After the dance lesson was over, they sat together at their small table, finishing their drinks. Val was regaling Doug and Jerry with stories of his time as a dancer, and from the point of view of rebuilding their business relationships, the evening had been a success.

But with Cara? With Cara his chest felt hot and tight. And wrong.

And when she stifled a yawn, he felt even worse. She was exhausted, still recovering from her surgery and she should get home. He stood.

Cara looked up at him and understood. She nodded.

They wished everyone a good evening and Teo ordered a car.

Neither of them spoke on the drive home. Was she also thinking of the dance? Of their conversation? Of the stories they told other people. Of the stories they told themselves, or could they leave all of that on the dance floor? He hoped so.

Once he'd let her into the house he looked at the staircase that led to his room, then turned back to Cara to wish her good-night.

'I think they all had a good time,' she said.

But did you? he wanted to ask.

What stories do you tell yourself?

That she had to keep moving. But she was so wrong. If only she could see that her grief was holding her back from all the happiness that she deserved.

'You don't have to keep running, you know,' he said. So much for leaving their conversation in the cantina where it belonged.

'What?' Confusion blinked over her face before she said, 'Oh, about before. I'm not.'

'You move around so much, it's almost like you're a fugitive.'

She laughed. 'Fugitives don't dress like this,' she said, and pointed to her red dress.

His mouth turned dry and he had to swallow hard. She was right. Everyone in the bar had noticed Cara and her dress.

'I've told you, I'm running towards the world. To new opportunities. Besides, you're one to talk.'

'What on earth do you mean?'

'Your games.'

He didn't play games. Especially not with women. He was always transparent about his intentions. Overly so. 'What games? I don't play games.'

'The games you *make*. And you do play them, you told me. It is literally your work.'

'It's hardly all my work. My work is the business to sell the games.'

'So, you sell games to allow people to slip into another world.'

'And why is that wrong? Books, movies, they all do the same thing.'

'You've just accused me of running away from something and yet I don't think you're living your best or fullest life either.'

'My life is great.' It was. His business was a success; his reputation was solid. He was a strong, contributing member of society. What was she talking about?

She shook her head. *'I can't get anything wrong. I can't make a mistake.* Sound familiar? That you will never repay Pablo. Teo, you don't owe Pablo anything.'

Stupid dance, stupid telling each other a story! What had possessed him? Either of them to open up to one another like that.

She stamped her foot, as she'd been taught earlier that evening, and he warmed at the memory of her stomping on his foot.

Cara let out an exasperated groan.

'What's the matter?' he asked.

'You. You're the matter, Teo.'

He shook his head. 'What about me?'

'I can't figure you out.'

'Cara, I'm an open book.' Especially after tonight. She'd practically seen into his soul.

She pulled back. 'No, you see, you're not at all. Not one little bit. I don't understand you at all.'

'I'm so simple, really.' It wasn't a lie. Not totally. Most of the time he was honest.

Except when it comes to Cara you're not. You're not even honest with yourself about how you feel. Because if you were honest you'd step up to her and take her in your arms.

His gut twisted. He wanted desperately to tell her the truth, but he could never be honest with her about that.

'You work so hard, yet you rarely enjoy it,' she said.

'That's not true.'

'Yes, it is true. And don't even get me started on the charity.'

'What is wrong with the charity?' His exasperation made him breathless.

Or maybe that was just Cara, now standing so

close to him he could see the freckles covering her nose.

'Nothing, nothing at all. It's wonderful. That's the point.'

'What? How is that the point?' he wondered.

'Because it's too generous.'

'How can something be too generous?'

'When you look after everyone else, but not yourself. And I don't understand why you asked me to stay, especially when you never liked me.'

'Now, that's not true at all. We talked about that.' They had dealt with this. As best as he could anyway. And besides, he did like her. Didn't she see that?

'Isn't it? You're hot and cold with me and it's confusing and not nice.'

He looked down, away from her eyes. Shame washed through him. She was right. Each time he let himself relax around her, he'd remember all the reasons he shouldn't and would pull away again.

You aren't honest with her.

If there was a button to press to make him feel about an inch tall, she'd found it. And pushed it. He had been distant with her, even stern. But he'd never wanted to be dishonest.

'Cara—' his voice cracked '—I don't mean to be.'

'Then why? Why are you like this?'

'You're going to make me say it?'

'Yes, because I don't understand.'

He couldn't say the words. Not even to himself. Instead, he stepped up to her, slid his hand into hers and squeezed. Would that small gesture be enough for her to understand?

She entwined her fingers in his but still looked up at him helplessly. How couldn't she understand? Surely it was written across his face. Surely everything about this evening had told her how he felt? The dance, the embrace? The breathless conversation they had shared in the middle of the dance floor. Surely she saw it in everything he said, everything he did.

No.

You've kept it so well hidden, most of all from yourself.

Cara moved closer. She squeezed his hand back and pressed her body softly again his. Her perfume swirled in the air around him like a spell drawing them together.

She tilted her face upwards, eyes wide open and pleading. 'Teo.' That was all she said. Not a question demanding an answer. Just his name. Her fingers squeezed his. His heart stopped.

Something shifted inside him.

You have to tell her the truth. How much you really want her.

He leant down in increments; she didn't pull away. She waited, watched him, until he could stand it no more, and closed his eyes and touched his mouth to hers. Her lips were warm and tasted sweet, floral, fragrant, just like her. The relief he felt when she opened her mouth and kissed him back was incendiary.

Cara lifted her hands to the back of his neck and grasped the hair at the nape. He slid his own hand into her hair, as he'd imagined doing more times than he cared to admit, and tilted her head so their mouths fit perfectly together. He'd longed to do this for an eternity, to take her, touch her, bury himself in her embrace. To have her do the same. To hear her sighs, to taste her mouth. To feel her heartbeat against his.

Her lips parted, her mouth and arms wide open and he fell into them, explored, tasted, wondered and lost himself completely. It was like coming home, desire fired up inside him.

More. He wanted more. He wanted all of it.

He wanted to scoop her up, carry her to his bed and kiss every inch of her. To feel her on him, to hear the sounds of her pleasure. To give himself to her. To lose himself completely.

'Teo, don't stop. Don't.' She tugged at his shirt and her fingers were like ice as they touched the burning flesh of his stomach.

No.

This is wrong.

He pulled back, gasped for breath.

Cara was also panting, but the look on her face was more than he could bare to see. She'd just accused him of being hot and cold, and in an effort to prove her wrong he'd proven her right.

'Cara, that was…too much.'

'Too much?'

'And that's why we can't go any further. I'm sorry.'

'You're sorry for kissing me or sorry we can't go any further?'

Cara knew words. She believed in using them correctly. There was no hiding his thought behind imprecise language.

'Maybe both. You and I…it would be too messy.'

Cara blinked. Reconfiguring. Processing. But was she relieved or upset? He couldn't tell. At that moment he barely knew his name.

She sniffed, nodded. 'You think we should forget that ever happened?'

He exhaled. 'I think that would be best.'

'Well, let me know how you go with that.' She raised an eyebrow, grasped his gaze in her golden eyes and held it captive in a long, challenging look.

His heart fell and he struggled for a retort. He struggled simply for breath.

'Good night.' Cara shrugged, turned and went down the corridor to her room.

Teo watched her go. Head held high, her hips swaying confidently.

He closed his eyes and rubbed them hard with

the palms of his hands, but his head still swirled with memories of that kiss. Heck, he could still taste her, his arms still tingled with the sensation of holding her.

She was right. Him forget that kiss?

Never.

CHAPTER EIGHT

It was morning and Cara's body was on fire. And not because during the time she'd been in Seville the spring had become summer, but because her core temperature had not dropped since last night. At some point she'd tossed off the bedsheets which were now just a tangled heap at the foot of her bed. Dancing with Teo had been hard enough, but the kiss.

That kiss! That kiss had ignited something inside her that was still burning out of control hours later. Teo had stepped up to her, waited almost long enough for her to beg and then pulled her into his arms. She wasn't sure exactly how or why, detail was lost to her, gone the way of her inhibitions and common sense, leaving only desire in its place. Desire that was still pulsating through her veins the next morning.

Desire mixed with a decent amount of resentment. How could he have lit that fire, fanned the flames and then stepped away with barely a shrug? Telling her that more was impossible. Leaving her flailing around unsatisfied. Scorched.

She was proud of her parting shot to Teo. Surprised she'd had it in her, when her bones felt like liquid and she wasn't sure which way was up.

More is impossible.

The one thing she wasn't, though, was confused. Last night explained Teo's strange behaviour. He was definitely attracted to her. No one with lukewarm feelings kissed like that. But Teo, hopelessly uptight Teo, he was the one who was confused. Not Cara.

A shower. She needed a shower. To start with.

But the cold water didn't tame the heat that still smouldered inside her.

A holiday fling was probably exactly what she needed. In fact, hadn't Dr Magdalena hinted as much when she'd told Cara to relax and enjoy Seville? When she'd told her that *all* activities were safe?

She had doctor's orders. Maybe she should tell Teo that? He was overly concerned with her well-being after all.

Cara smirked to herself and slipped a dress over her head.

She might not have had many relationships, but she did have a few friends with benefits scattered around the globe. People who she knew and had built up trust with, but who were only after the same thing she was: safe sex with a trusted person who didn't want anything more. Someone who shared her desire to remain unattached.

And Teo, surprisingly, seemed to fit this bill. In the past few weeks she had come to trust him, she was attracted to him and, like her, he was a loner. He wasn't looking for a relationship any more than she was. Cara looked at herself in the mirror. Yes, a fling was exactly what she needed. Let's face it. It was probably exactly what Teo needed as well.

Now the idea had occurred to her, it consumed her. She loved a challenge. And Teo was a challenge like no other. She smiled even more. This was going to be fun.

It was never because I didn't like you.

Teo did like her, but at some point, he must have determined that she was off-limits.

Because of Pablo? That had to be it. He was overly preoccupied with Pablo and with doing the right thing by him. Not to mention his almost pathological need to never make mistakes.

And yet, what she wanted from Teo was nothing like what she'd had with Pablo. She and Pablo had both been so young, so full of optimism and romance and hope.

But she and Teo were two flawed souls who were very physically compatible and in the same city for a while. Teo didn't need to worry that she would want anything more. That wasn't what she was after and not what she was offering.

Looking at her reflection, Cara changed her mind and took off her dress and bra. She wrapped her robe around herself, pulled it tight, then loosened the tie so it hung just a little too loose. This was her game and she could make up the rules.

'Good morning,' she announced brightly, entering the kitchen. Teo looked up and smiled, but the tightness around his lips indicated it was forced. Seeing him struggle only made her smile more.

Teo might pride himself on not playing games but she was happy to. She had set him a challenge to forget the kiss and what fun was a challenge if it was easy? She was going to make sure that while she was around, he never forgot that he'd been the one to wrap her in his arms and take her mouth.

'Did you sleep well?' she asked.

Teo had already made a pot of coffee and laid the table with bread, cheeses and fruit. She picked up a strawberry, opened her mouth for a beat too long before slowly placing the strawberry in it. Teo's jaw tensed, just for an instant, and he looked away.

She sat next to him at the large kitchen table, not across from him as she'd been accustomed to. He acknowledged her new position but shifted his chair slightly in the opposite direction. She held back a laugh.

'What's on today?' she asked.

'Nothing with the producers, they have meetings with their studio, so you can have a day off.'

That was good and bad. Days off were great, but a day away from Teo stewing about last night?

'Great!' she said cheerfully. 'I might have an explore, revisit some old haunts.'

At that comment, Teo's face darkened. They both knew what old haunts entailed. Rule one of the game must be 'Don't mention Pablo.'

'Good idea.' Teo's voice was gruff.

'But I think both of us have exhausted our cooking abilities. Why don't I let you take me out for dinner?'

She saw the expressions change on Teo's face, from aloofness to mild amusement, to something resembling relief? Or dread? Like a man who knew his fate.

'I know just the place.' Teo stood and pushed in his chair.

'I'm looking forward to it.' She smiled as sweetly as she could, though her intentions were anything but.

Let me know how you go with forgetting that kiss.

'Don't work too hard,' she yelled after him as he left the kitchen.

Yes. The dance was on. And this time she would take the lead.

Cara caught a cab back to the shopping district. She spent the morning going from shop to shop to find just the right dress, and after a few stores she found it. A deep, luscious pink. The colour of her lips.

It had a halter neckline, and dipped low into her chest. It showed exactly the right amount of skin, but the straps wouldn't cover any bra she owned, so she'd need new lingerie. The shop assistant pointed her in the direction of a lingerie boutique where she couldn't decide which bra looked best so she bought both and matching underwear. And her black sandals wouldn't do the dress justice so she needed shoes as well and the shop assistant in the lingerie shop sent her in the direction of a shoe shop.

Shopping was fun, dressing up was too. She couldn't take all these clothes with her, but maybe she could ship some back to Hannah's place in New Jersey.

Because what if the lawyers had good news for her? What if she *could* get her house back? Then she'd have a whole wardrobe to store these dresses.

One day.

Maybe one day.

Oh no.

Cara stood at the bottom of the staircase waiting for him. She clutched a small bag and he tried to focus his attention on that, or on her fingers, because looking anywhere else made his heart thump in his throat and his brain short-circuit.

She was wearing a dress he hadn't seen on her before.

Pink. Dark, dusty pink. A colour that suggested all kinds of other places. It's shape too, every one of her curves were hinted at, all the places he shouldn't want to kiss.

Let me know how you go with that.

He focused on her shoes, strappy sandals with a small heel. An even darker pink.

Heaven help him.

He'd chosen a bar not far from the house. It was a small neighbourhood place that he didn't visit often enough. Only when they arrived did he curse his choice. It was small, intimate, bathed in the glow of candles and small lamps that made the light in the room a warm, cosy red.

He had to stop it. So she was wearing pink? So what if she looked gorgeous? He'd seen beautiful women in pink before and hadn't reacted like this. He had to pull himself together, he was stronger than this.

She deferred to him to order, 'You know what's good,' and she passed him her menu but their hands brushed in the process, sending the usual sparks skipping up his arm.

They ordered spicy potatoes, mushroom rice, and chickpea and chorizo stew. Half a carafe of wine only. They didn't need to linger over this meal. Not when she seemed determined to break him.

The bar had velvet bench seats, red and as seductive as the lighting. He foolishly chose one in the corner, thinking it would give them more space, but when a couple arrived at a neighbouring table Cara smiled at them before scooting along on the bench seat until she was a breath away, their thighs close enough to bump with each movement.

She's playing with you. That's what she's doing. The casual touches, her tongue lingering on her lips. All of it.

Let me know how you go with that.

She was challenging him, but why? She had loved Pablo, surely any sort of physical relationship with Teo should be off-limits to her as much as it was to him.

'Do you still think about Pablo?' he asked. It was one of those questions that sounded better in his head.

Cara sucked in a quick breath. They had spoken occasionally about Pablo, his name was no longer taboo, yet he realised too late that his question sounded like an accusation and he hadn't meant it as that. He'd only meant to remind her of the person who stood between them and the flirtatious game she was playing.

'I'm sorry,' he added quickly. 'That came out completely wrong. What I meant was…'

She shook her head. 'It's okay, I get it. You're wondering how I'm feeling about him, how I feel about being in Seville. If I miss him.'

Teo nodded, grateful for her generous interpretation of his question.

'We've hardly talked about him,' she continued. 'And that's partly my fault. I can see he's still such a big part of your life, with the business, the charity. It's like he lives alongside you. That's been hard.'

'I didn't mean to suggest that you don't think about him.'

'But that's the thing, sometimes I don't. And it's not because I don't love him, or because I don't miss him, but because I couldn't function if I thought about him every day. The same goes for my parents.'

His chest, which had been tight with tension, now cracked. Oh, Cara. To have suffered so much loss by the time she was barely in her twenties. No one deserved that, least of all someone as lovely as she. And now he'd inconsiderately brought it all up.

'I love them, I miss them every day, but I can't let it bury me. I have to let it sit with me, walk alongside me. I'm sorry if that sounds heartless, but it's how I cope.'

He shook his head. 'It's not heartless. It's practical.'

She snorted. 'It's necessary. Circumstance has

left me on my own, with only myself to rely on, so I have to get on with it. I don't have the luxury of letting it consume me, so instead I live with it. None of them would want me to spend my whole life mourning them.'

'You've never met anyone else?' Teo anticipated the answer to this question but asked it, nonetheless.

With a single shake of her head she said, 'That's another thing entirely. Being able to manage my grief is one thing, but setting myself up for more is entirely another.'

So their loss still affected her, just not in the ways he'd assumed.

He had managed his grief differently, pouring himself into Verdadero, and then the foundation. His grief for Pablo impacted his life every day, but it wasn't a problem.

Isn't it? Isn't it holding you back? Stopping you from acknowledging your needs? Your desires? The beautiful woman sitting in front of you now?

With a single shake of his head he said, 'Grief is very personal, individual. I'm sorry again if I suggested yours was nothing.'

'It's okay, really. You loved Pablo too, you've dedicated your life to his memory. It's admirable, it really is. I don't know how you did it, living with him every day, with his ideas, his characters.'

The food and wine arrived like a saviour and

he mulled over her words. She wasn't looking for a relationship. At least not to fall in love. That confession made him relax somewhat. She was only flirting with him, having fun. He didn't need to be so suspicious or jumpy. They compared notes as they ate, and for a moment all mention of Pablo was forgotten. As they finished eating, he reached for the carafe to pour them another glass of wine just as Cara happened to reach for it as well. She held up her hands to surrender the drink to him and he poured them both a glass.

'Thank you,' she said with a smile. As if to push the point home, she placed her hand on his thigh. Any moment now and he'd be a goner.

'You loved Pablo, didn't you?'

'Of course. I don't see what that's got to do with anything.'

Teo looked down at her hand on his knee.

She continued. 'I did love him. I was very young when we met, and it was a long time ago. Do you understand what I'm saying?'

Teo shook his head.

'I haven't been a nun.'

Oh.

His mouth went dry. His throat as well. The painful tightness spread through his entire body.

'Are you shocked? Upset?' she asked.

'No, of course not,' he spluttered.

'You look shocked.'

'I'm only shocked that you are *telling* me. Your private life is truly none of my business.'

She shrugged so subtly he doubted anyone else would've noticed.

'I feel you should know.'

But why? He'd never ask a woman about her sex life. Why was it any of his business? Because he'd be upset on Pablo's behalf?

He thought carefully about his next words, and even whether her statement needed a response. He eventually settled on 'I'm sure Pablo would've wanted you to move on.'

'Precisely,' she said.

Yet that still didn't explain why she was telling him.

'But you still look disapproving.'

'I don't disapprove at all. I'm happy for you,' he said, but the way he clenched his jaw and swallowed with an audible gulp suggested otherwise. How could he possibly tell her that it wasn't anything to do with Pablo, but the thought of her being with other men made every cell in his body freeze and sicken.

She laughed. 'You're a terrible actor.'

'I know,' he said. 'Anything artistic or creative, you can forget it.' He didn't have Pablo's talents or his family's. He was boring, traditional.

Cara narrowed her eyes and grinned.

'I haven't fallen in love with anyone else. It's

not as though I've settled down with anyone. It's just sex,' she said.

'I'm not judging. I'm happy for you. Truly.' He pushed his empty wine glass away.

'I'm not going to break, Teo,' she whispered.

'I know, you're recovered. The doctor said.'

'Not my body. Teo, I'm talking about my heart. You aren't going to hurt me.'

And he understood. Cara was proposing something physical, not emotional. Her heart wasn't on the line. Their hearts, their feelings would be safe.

And as the warmth of her palm spread into his leg and worked its inevitable way up into his body, he believed her.

They could do this. They could give in to their attraction and it wouldn't be wrong.

That's what she was saying. He looked back at her and caught the sparkle in her eyes.

'Are you sure?'

She smiled. 'Yes, I'm sure. I like you, Teo, but as you said last night, you and I would be too messy. But I'm not talking about a romance, I'm talking about a fling. Between two consenting adults. While I'm in Seville.'

The smile that spread across her face showed her she knew what his answer was going to be before he'd even admitted it to himself.

How could he refuse her anything? Her heart wasn't in danger and so nor would his be. With that certainty, he did something he'd been longing to for days. He picked up her hand and rested it on his. Then he stoked her fingers with his thumb, looked at her pink nails, studied the softness of her skin. He turned her hand over and did the same with her palm, getting to know every crease, every pore, her hand slack in his, as she watched him study her, let him take his time. Then his quest went higher, up her arm, its silky-smooth skin, and to the bare skin of her shoulder that had been driving him to distraction all night. Her shoulder, the fading tan line, the single freckle proving she was real and not a flawless icon. Cara sighed, softly, silently but he saw her shoulders fall and felt her sweet breath mingle with his.

He pressed his lips to her shoulder, then worked a trail of kisses up over her collarbone and her neck until he tasted the spot behind her ear. Cara moaned and he was inspired. Teo pressed his lips against hers, carefully, thoughtfully, measuring each caress, like he was putting the final touches to a piece of art. Suddenly, she lifted her hand to the side of his head, turned his mouth to hers and took him completely. The force of her desire knocked the air from his lungs and the hesitation from his mind.

When he lost sensation in his knees and pulled her tighter, Cara, sensibly, pulled her mouth half an inch from his and sighed. 'I think we should move somewhere more comfortable, don't you?'

Teo went to the bar and paid and Cara followed, not moving more than a foot from his side.

CHAPTER NINE

CARA'S BODY WAS aflame by the time they got back to Teo's, pressed flush to the front door of the pink house. He fumbled with the key, but she couldn't keep her hands off him, ran them over his shoulders down his arms, which only caused him to fumble the key even more. Even once the key was in the lock, his shaking hand still struggled to turn it as she pressed kisses to the back of his neck and slid her fingers through his dark hair. Excitement, relief and joy all fought for supremacy in her body. When the door finally pushed open, they fell inside and she sought out the full attention of his mouth. She was vaguely aware of him kicking the front door closed, only slightly noticing the noise it made. All her focus, all her attention was on him, his lips, his hands and her own struggle to undo the buttons to free his body from his clothes.

'My room,' she mumbled because the stairs at that point seemed like an insurmountable hurdle for her legs, which were rapidly losing tension.

Teo didn't argue, keeping his lips on hers as they shuffled down the corridor to her room.

Her mattress when they reached it was like a relief. An oasis. His shirt came away easily from his shoulders and back, his trousers, even more so. But he struggled with her dress. The straps were tied in a tight knot at the back 'This dress will be the death of me,' he said.

Wait until he sees what's underneath it, she thought.

She knew the moment that he had from the groan that left his body. The lacey bra, the almost non-existent underwear she had purchased to wear underneath it. Worth every penny.

'I'm never going to be able to forget these, you do know that don't you?' he mumbled as he kissed her neck.

'That may or may not have been my intention,' she said as she glided her hand down his underpants, feeling her way around him, exploring what lay beneath them. Before sliding her hand inside as she watched the look on his face change from excitement to the grimace of delighted pain. Cara ran her hands over the light hair on his hard chest, brought her lips to his nipples and felt his body tense beneath them.

She loved every moment of this, every sound, every touch, every ripple of desire that shivered through her and took her breath further and further away.

She caught her breath as Teo fumbled for his wallet and protection. She took the packet from his trembling hands and ripped it open herself. Her fingers were only slightly less shaky than his and as she sheathed him, he covered her hands with his, stilling her. Holding his breath.

'Cara, are you sure?'

'Oh, Teo, I've never been more certain.' Cara pulled Teo's strong frame back to her, every part of her aching, needy and ready. He kissed her lips, her neck, her breasts and she cried out.

'Now, Teo, please now.'

When they finally came together, Teo sucked in a deep breath and held it as she began to move. Finally, finally she felt him relax and move with her, rubbing and pressing all the right places, saw the concentration on his beautiful face.

He broke seconds after her.

He's been waiting. He's been waiting for you.

Cara rested her head on Teo's chest. With his arm around her, holding her snuggly against him she felt herself drifting back to sleep. He really did make the most relaxing pillow.

Teo shifted and placed a kiss against her forehead. 'I hate to do this but we need to get up. I've got meetings.'

Teo rolled away and she groaned. He was too comfortable; this bed was her new favourite place. Teo pulled on a pair of shorts.

'I'm going to be as quick as I can and then I'll come right back here, I promise.'

Cara rolled onto her back and groaned again. She had to get up too; she'd agreed to take the producers to the Alcázar. It wasn't an official part of her job but she'd offered to play tour guide to help keep the relationship on track while Teo and Val attended to some of their other work. She'd been pleased when Doug and Jerry had accepted. But that had been yesterday. Before.

Before she knew what making love with Teo would actually be like. And to be fair, if she'd known all along the kind of things Teo could do with his fingers, let alone his tongue, she wouldn't have been able to get anything done for the past few weeks.

'I need coffee. If you're going to keep me up all night, you'll need to make me a bucket.'

'Oh, I kept you up? I thought it was the other way around.'

He knelt back on the bed and kissed her again. Cara opened her mouth and deepened the kiss, pulling him back to her, but he pulled away.

She groaned again but this time, got up. If Teo was leaving the room there was no point in her staying. She grabbed her robe and pulled it around herself, with nothing underneath. Maybe she could convince him to come back to bed for a short while before they left for the day. But after some coffee. Her body was relaxed, boneless and happier than it had been in months, still buzzing from the places he'd taken her last night.

Cara followed Teo out of the bedroom, still thinking about the things he'd done. She wasn't paying attention and walked straight into the kitchen before she realised that the room already smelt of coffee. And eggs. And fresh bread.

The table was already laid and Alba was at the sink.

'Oh, good morning to you both.' She smiled at Teo, who was wearing only shorts and Cara in an open robe that she hastily tied up. Alba didn't look the slightest bit surprised, let alone shocked.

'We got back late last night. I thought I messaged you, but I realised this morning the message didn't go through,' she explained.

'It's…' Teo stumbled over his words and the back of his neck reddened.

'This looks great, thank you,' Cara said, sitting down. 'How's your daughter? I was getting very worried. She's been ill for *so* long.'

'She's so much better, thank you. But then it went through the entire house.'

Cara wondered if they'd ever know the truth. Teo certainly thought Alba's absence was contrived. It was a remarkable coincidence that she'd returned this morning. Of all mornings.

'I hope you've been managing. I'm so sorry to leave while you were staying.'

'We've been managing just fine,' Teo said, sitting with his back straight, his jaw tight. He had changed back to old Teo. Proper Teo. Professional Teo.

'Yes, we've muddled through,' Cara confirmed, trying not to laugh.

Alba left the kitchen, not even bothering to hide her own smirk.

Cara put her hand on Teo's strong thigh and squeezed. 'Relax, it's just Alba. Besides, I bet she knew this was going to happen before we did.' Cara pointed back and forth between them.

Teo leant closer. 'You know it's not that simple,' he said.

'I know.' She did know what he meant. It was Teo's pathological need for propriety. 'But it also isn't complicated either. This, you and me, we both know it's just for while I'm here. We know it's nothing more than that. Who cares what she thinks?'

'It isn't Alba I'm worried about. You're my employee.'

'Only until the deal with the producers is finished.'

'But still.' Teo buttered his bread with such force he ripped a hole in it.

'You don't want anyone to know? About us?' She asked the question but was then, suddenly, afraid of the answer.

'I want to shout it from the rooftops,' he whispered. 'But I don't think that would do either of our professional reputations any favours if our personal relationship became common knowledge.'

Cara blushed at the thought of Teo standing on his roof yelling to the entire square and the streets beyond that they had made love. She'd think more about that image later, but he was right. Discretion was not a bad idea. He wasn't suggesting secrecy, just caution.

'Yes, that's true.' The chances of any of her clients finding out about her relationship with Teo were slim but not non-existent, and she preferred to keep her professional and personal lives as separate as possible.

'And it wouldn't look great for the deal if the producers found out,' Teo said.

'I doubt it would be fatal, but it wouldn't be a good look.'

She understood exactly where he was coming from, maintaining professional appearances was important to her but even more so to Teo.

'So you're okay if we keep this, not secret, but discreet?' he asked.

'Yes, that's sensible. And besides, what is there to tell? We're two consenting adults enjoying one another's company. It's no one else's business.' She leant towards him and kissed his cheek. Her entire body sighed. He smelt and tasted wonderful. She wanted to devour him and not the breakfast laid carefully out in front of them.

She kissed him again.

After a cursory glance at the door, he kissed her back.

It was an effort to pull away from the kiss. Even more of an effort to get ready for the day. Teo kept pulling away to go up to his room to change but Cara nudged him back with kisses and caresses and talk about what she was planning to do to him when they got home that afternoon. They compromised, agreeing to another kiss once they were both dressed. And again once they were out the door.

By the time they arrived at the Verdadero offices in the luxury Torre Sevilla building, they were both late for their appointments. And she didn't care at all. She should care, after all she was invested in the deal going through as well. Maybe not as much as Teo, but she'd be devastated if it didn't get over the line. So when he parked the car in the underground car park and reached over for another kiss, she held him back with a hand.

Doug and Jerry were waiting for her in the expansive Verdadero reception area, but had coffees in front of them and were chatting away with Teo's assistant, Amaia.

'I'm so sorry, the traffic was awful this morning,' Cara explained, but happily Doug and Jerry didn't seem concerned.

The three of them took a car to the Real Alcázar, the stunning royal palace in the heart of historic Seville. Amaia had booked them skip-the-queue tickets.

The Alcázar was the first place Cara had visited on her first trip to Seville and had been awed by the history and the beauty of the medieval Islamic palace. It was no different this time around, the detailed lattice work, the colourful mosaics, stunning tapestries, each room and courtyard more stunning than the last.

They were standing in the Hall of Ambassadors admiring the magnificent golden dome, when another sight knocked the breath out of her: Teo striding towards them, a smile on his usually reserved face.

She wanted to reach for him and sensed his hand moving towards hers but they both held back.

'What are you doing here? I thought you had meetings,' she asked.

'They finished earlier than expected.' He smiled and she wondered for a second if he was telling the truth. He had to be, surely. Mateo Ortiz would never play hooky. Or lie.

He greeted the producers with another smile and the four of them completed the trip around the palace, with Teo pointing out the different architectural styles, small facts only locals would know, his pride in his city apparent to all.

A hand brush when no one was looking. A

knowing smile. An 'accidental' bump. Her body was burning up by the time Jerry suggested lunch and the four of them sat down at a nearby restaurant.

Jerry claimed the seat next to her and Doug opposite, leaving her crestfallen even though she knew it was probably for the best. Teo was charming but it was an effort to keep her mind on the conversation and off the man speaking. And how he looked without his clothes. And the sounds he'd made. And the look on his face when he had made her climax for the second time. And the third.

Cara had to be alerted back to the present when it was time to leave, so distracted she'd been by memories of the previous night.

'I'd better get back to the office,' Teo said, and she tried to ignore her disappointment. 'Can I give you gentlemen a lift?'

Doug and Jerry declined the offer and left Teo and Cara outside the restaurant. Once she was sure they'd turned the corner out of sight, she finally, finally, picked up Teo's hand. Strong, comforting, exciting. She stepped up to him. Their bodies separated by a whisper. 'It's a shame you have to go back to the office,' she said.

'I don't,' he whispered into her ear, sending a thrill down her body.

'But you said…'

'I fibbed. I don't have any commitments this afternoon.'

'None?'

'Well, just one.' He smiled and oh how she loved seeing Teo smile. 'I have a commitment to you.' He pressed his mouth against the side of her neck and her insides leapt, wild with anticipation.

A week later Teo sat in his office, staring at the papers on the desk in front of him. It might have been a week, he wasn't sure. Days and nights had blurred together in an erotic, exciting mix. He was awake in the night, asleep in the day. He didn't know what was up and down any longer. The only thing that kept him centred was Cara. Everything seemed to begin and end with her.

Except this contract. This deal. That was now in front of him and had been for hours. Or was it minutes? He was no longer sure of anything.

Particularly his own feelings.

I'm not going to break. You won't hurt me, Teo.

But what about me? Am I *going to hurt me?*

No. He wasn't. They had agreed their relationship was physical only. Not to mention short-term. They were old friends who shared an unbreakable bond. But it wasn't more than that. What Teo was feeling was happiness and joy. And the endorphin rush that came from having a lot of very good sex. It wasn't nothing, but it wasn't more than that.

Val sauntered into Teo's office without saying a word, much less knocking. This was normal for Val. If you happened to be looking for him, the last place you would ever check would be Val's own office.

'What's up?' Val asked, sitting in his usual chair.

'I'm just looking over the final contract. It seems to be all there, but something's still bugging me.'

'Teo, it looks great. The lawyers have looked over it ten times, you've gone over it twenty. Sign it. Celebrate!'

He pressed his lips together. 'No. Something's off. I'll figure it out.'

'Could it be the fact that once you sign this contract, the lovely Cara will be leaving Seville?'

Teo scoffed. 'She was always going to leave. That was always the plan.' The studio had put some loophole in the contract somewhere. There must be a typo or two to find. *Something.* If he'd been paying closer attention, instead of daydreaming about Cara, he would have found it by now.

'But I don't think the plan was for you to become so close to her either.'

Teo didn't like what Val was suggesting. He and Cara had been very discreet, not even Val would have picked up what was going on between them.

'You've become close to her too,' Teo said.

Val laughed. 'Sure, but not in the same way you have.'

He should deny it, but the weight had been pressing so heavily on him he couldn't, and what was the harm if Val already seemed to know?

'Say, theoretically, if you wanted to date your dead friend's ex-girlfriend, what would be the problems with that?'

'If by *your dead friend*, you mean Pablo, who has been dead for ten years and if by *ex-girlfriend*, you mean Cara, then nothing except your own complexes.'

'That's not true.' It wouldn't be right. It would *never* be right.

Val's face turned from amused to serious. He rose and walked to Teo's desk and stood next to him, forcing him to look up. Val placed his hands on Teo's shoulders.

'Pablo is gone and not even recently. Apart from anything else, you've spent the last ten years dedicating your life to his work and building an institution in his name. No one could accuse you of doing anything wrong as far as Pablo is concerned.'

'But this is Cara. The love of his life.'

'And so what? Did you ever wonder if it could actually be a good thing?'

'How?' Teo's voice was strangled. He was betraying his friend. And not just anyone, but Pablo, who had been the first person to accept him after his father's crimes. Who had trusted him with his creations.

'Because wouldn't Pablo have wanted her to be with someone he loved and respected?' Val asked.

Would he? Each time Teo let himself think something like that, he'd wonder if it weren't simply wishful thinking. Pablo had loved Cara so much, wouldn't it break his heart to know that Teo had stepped in?

Val continued. 'Besides, what Pablo might have thought is irrelevant—because he's not here. And apart from anything else, what Pablo may or may not have thought is hardly the most important thing.'

'What is?'

'Oh, Teo, I despair of you. I'm hardly a relationship guru, but seriously?'

If it were so obvious that Val—terminally single Val—could see it, then how low had Teo sunk?

'The most important thing is how she feels. How does she feel?'

'She thinks it should just be a temporary thing.' Teo sighed. Cara's heart was not for winning.

Val raised an eyebrow. 'Interesting.'

'Is it? How? It suggests to me that the whole thing is impossible.'

Val smiled. 'It suggests to me that you have done more than just think about how you feel.

When did she say that she thought it should be temporary? At the beginning?'

'Yes. We were honest with one another when we…um, started.'

Val bit back a smirk. 'And since then?'

'Well, no. Because the deal was that it would be temporary.'

'Sometimes deals change. This started as one movie and turned into the option of three.' Val pointed to the papers on Teo's desk.

'It's not the same.'

'No, but it's not that different.'

Teo snorted. 'This is a business contract, I'm talking about…' He couldn't even say the words. Love. A relationship. Commitment. How could Val even compare what was in Teo's chest to the papers in front of him.

One was just a deal. A big one, but still just a deal.

Cara was so much more than that. Teo wanted to bury his face in his palms and sob.

But he couldn't, not even in front of Val.

How had he got himself into this situation? How had he managed to get himself into a place where he was falling for Cara? Where he was risking absolutely everything. His reputation, their business, and most of all, his heart.

'But, Pablo,' Teo said.

'Pablo would be happy for you both! Ah, it isn't

Pablo you're worried about, is it? It's what everything else will think.'

'No.' *Yes.*

'You're worried people will think it's wrong. That people will think less of you. That they will think you've betrayed your friend.'

'I can't afford to ruin my reputation. *You* can't afford for me to ruin my reputation.' Their employees couldn't afford for him to do that. The millions of children supported by programs run by the Pablo Pascal Foundation couldn't either.

Val laughed. 'I think both our reputations can withstand you being in a consensual, mutually caring relationship. The only thing you have to worry about is what Cara thinks.'

Val was logical. Calculating. Mathematical, but what did he know about relationships? He was just as clueless as Teo.

Besides, Cara thought it was temporary. And he couldn't ask her, because what if that made her uncomfortable? He didn't want to ruin any chance of an ongoing connection and if he reneged on their agreement, he'd be doing that.

There was a knock at the door and both men turned. It was Cara, looking gorgeous in a plain black suit, her hair tied back and a lick of red lipstick. Her professional outfit. She thought it made her blend into the background but, as far as Teo was concerned, when she was in the room the rest of the world fell away.

Even if she wasn't in the same room as him, just the thought of her had the same effect.

'I'm about to head home and just wanted to let you know,' Cara said.

'Come in, Cara, come in.' Val gestured for her to enter.

Teo had a bad feeling about what was going to come next.

'How are you enjoying Seville?' Val asked but he might as well have hired a skywriter to tell Cara he knew about their relationship.

Cara looked from Teo and back to Val. 'Just fine?' she answered.

'Great, great. And where are you heading next?'

'Brussels. My next job is lined up for next week.'

'That's terrific, you'll be able to come to the ball after all.'

'The ball?'

'You know, for the foundation. It's this Saturday. Five days from now.'

'Oh, I don't...'

'You don't what? You are coming, aren't you?'

'I...' She looked back to Teo and the confusion on his face.

They hadn't revisited this conversation since early in Cara's stay when Val had first brought it up.

'You should come.' Teo's voice was rough.

She narrowed her eyes, as well she should. That was not a way to issue an invitation. Because he hadn't intended to ask her. He hadn't intended for her to come. The ball was about the foundation, which of course was all about Pablo.

'It's alright, I don't have to. If you don't want me to.'

'Of course I want you to. I didn't mention it earlier because I thought you would have left Seville by now. But you should definitely come.' Did he sound sincere enough?

If she came to the ball, she'd naturally be his plus-one. And then everyone would know that he was dating Pablo's ex. The thought made a bitter taste in his throat. And yet he was still foolish and selfish enough to want her there.

Val's invitation was far more generous. 'Of course you should come. I won't accept no for an answer. And if Teo hasn't asked you already, you can be my plus-one!'

They both looked at him, Cara's face was confused and hurt, Val's amused. Cara go to the ball, but with Val. Teo's throat constricted. It was unthinkable.

'Saturday night, shall I pick you up?' Val asked her.

'No need. Cara can come with me,' Teo said, then quickly turned to Cara, his face aflame. 'If you would like to come with me, I'd be honoured.'

'Thank you, I'd love to,' Cara said, not quite able to meet his eye.

Val clapped his hands. 'Fantastic, it'll be a great night.'

Cara looked between the two men, still uncertain, and nodded.

'Okay, good night. I'll see you back at home,' she said to Teo.

They both watched her leave. Val at least had the decency not to say anything more.

Teo stayed at the office much longer than he had been lately, far longer than he needed to. It was nearly eight when he arrived home. Cara was sitting in the living room, the television was on low and she turned when he entered.

'I'm sorry I'm late.'

'No need to apologise, you don't owe me an explanation.'

'Except I do. I was finalising the deal. Signing it.' He pulled a bottle of champagne out from behind his back. A peace offering and because Val was right, it was worth celebrating.

Cara whooped and ran to him. 'Congratulations! That's great news.'

'Yes, it is.'

'Yet you don't seem happy.'

'No, I am happy. I'm often like this, when a deal it done. It's somehow anticlimactic.'

'And you're worried about whether there are things you missed. Things you didn't think of?'

She knew him so well. How had that happened after only a few weeks?

It hadn't even been a month. It felt like no time at all and yet he also couldn't remember what his life was like before he'd received the phone call from the hospital.

He opened the bottle and Cara found the glasses. Working together as always.

'To Hollywood.' She touched his glass to hers.

'To Hollywood.' He sipped the wine and the bubbles hit him with a realisation: This was nice. It was good to celebrate with someone, even in a low-key way like this.

Especially if it were a low-key celebration like this.

'You've done such an amazing thing,' she said.

'We couldn't have done it without you.'

'I don't mean this deal. I mean the whole thing. Verdadero. The charity.'

'It's all Pablo's.'

'Are you mad? It isn't Pablo. It's you. And Val as well, but the way the company has been managed, the way you've steered it, that is all you.'

He shook his head,

'Are you being modest or do you truly not believe what I'm saying? Be honest.'

'Neither. The first game was designed by

Pablo. And the coding, all the software development, that was down to Val.'

'So, you're saying that Val and Pablo on their own, created all of this?' She opened her arms wide. 'You think Val could have done this deal on his own? Any of it?'

'Well, a lot of it.'

She smiled. 'I adore Val, he's undoubtedly brilliant, but he can't organise his way out of a paper bag. This is all *your* doing.'

'We're a team.'

'Okay, but you're a very important part of the team. Essential in fact.'

Teo had never allowed himself to believe he was successful. He was a helper, a facilitator, because the sons of criminals didn't get to be successful. The sons of liars had to try ten times as hard as anyone else to be trusted.

They sat on the sofa together and drank the champagne.

'I'm sorry you were forced to invite me to the ball,' she said.

Teo shook his head. 'Not at all.'

'Answer me this, then, am I going, or going *with* you to the ball?'

He tried to pretend he didn't know what she was getting at. 'We'll go together.'

She raised a pointed eyebrow. 'I don't have to go, you know.'

'Of course you do.'

'I don't want to go if you don't want me to go with you. It wasn't part of our arrangement.'

Their arrangement. Val was so wrong. Cara did still expect them to stick to their original deal. A physical relationship. While she was in Seville. That was all. Their arrangement didn't involve going as his date to a very public event.

'Of course I want you to be there.'

That was the truth, he did want her there, at his side. The problem was the thought of it also made him squirm.

'Will I embarrass you?' she said softly.

'What? No! Cara, no. It isn't that. Look, I know I haven't been as open about the ball as I should have been. It's only because I don't want things to be awkward for you.'

'Why would they be?'

'Pablo's parents will be there.'

Her shoulders dropped. 'Oh, I see. No, it's okay, I've actually been meaning to get in touch with them.'

'I didn't want to upset you. I know you loved him.'

'Yes, but it's in the past. If anything, I think going would give me a sense of closure. And… why are you really so keen to talk me out of it?'

'I'm honestly not. I didn't want to bring Pablo up, shove him in your face. The charity is dedicated to him after all.'

She laid her hand on his arm, a simple act but

he felt as though she controlled him completely. He could no more push her hand away than fly to the moon.

'I don't want to promise you anything I can't give you.' Teo's throat was tight.

She nodded.

'I don't want to hurt you, not ever. I want to be honest with you.'

'And I appreciate that,' she said.

'And going public with our relationship, well, we talked about that, didn't we?'

'At the beginning. Yes. And I suppose nothing's changed?'

'Of course things have changed,' he said.

Everything had changed. She'd upended his life. But in a week, she'd be gone. That was the arrangement.

'Like what?' her eyes sparkled.

'Like you are recovered from your surgery.'

'That's true.' She nodded.

'And I now do this.' He pressed his mouth to hers.

Cara melted into his arms. Some things had changed. Even he had a little. But had they changed enough to make her want to stay?

CHAPTER TEN

TEO TOOK THE empty glasses and champagne bottle in one hand and Cara's hand in the other. He tugged her off the sofa and towards the staircase.

'Upstairs?' she asked.

'Can you manage?'

'Of course, I might have weeks ago.' But she hadn't asked and he hadn't offered. Downstairs had everything she'd ever needed—her room, the kitchen, the comfy living room and the formal living room, and Teo's study. Downstairs was already a massive house.

Upstairs was Teo's private domain and she sensed, like his heart, that wasn't something he was ready to trust her with yet. If he ever would be.

'I was beginning to wonder if you have your first wife locked up here.'

Teo's mouth gaped.

She laughed. 'It's a reference from *Jane Eyre*.'

'Ah, I haven't read it. It doesn't feature too

prominently on Spanish school curricula,' he said as he led her upstairs.

'The hero, Mr Rochester, has locked his mentally ill wife upstairs in his mansion. Jane only finds out after she agrees to marry him when she's at the altar.'

While recounting the plot of *Jane Eyre*, Cara surreptitiously checked out the hidden story of this house.

'I'll give you the tour, if you like. You can check the bedrooms for ex-wives. So, he imprisoned one woman and then tried to marry another? And he's the hero? They end up together?'

'Yep.'

'Even though he locked up his wife, she forgave him?'

'It's a two-hundred-year-old story. But yes. I guess people forgive a lot of things.'

'But *that*?'

The upper floor also circumnavigated the courtyard below. Cara counted three or four large empty rooms. Each time Teo opened a door Cara said, 'Hello? Anyone here?'

Finally, he opened the door to the one room that did seem to be occupied.

The room had high ceilings and arched windows. It was open and airy yet still welcoming and comfortable, with white furnishings and dark exposed beams on the roof. The light was low, only a single lamp lit the entire room, bathing it in a seductive red glow.

Teo entered but she stood on the threshold. This was Teo's room, his own space.

'You have a lot of bedrooms,' she said. It was all she could think to say. She didn't want to dwell on the fact that once she walked into Teo's room something would change. She wasn't sure what, only that something would. Teo was trusting her with his own space.

He shrugged. 'They came with the house.'

She counted two, three large rooms. This was a house built for a family.

'What do you think you'll do with them? Do you think one day you might have children?'

'It isn't something I've thought much about. I can't quite imagine it.'

She bit her lip. She thought she felt the same way, but these empty rooms bothered her in a way she couldn't put her finger on.

'Do you think…you will ever have children?' he asked.

'I don't know, also I haven't really thought very much about it.'

Only theoretically. Only in the way you might think about winning the lottery. Or travelling into space. Things that were possible, yet seemingly highly unlikely to happen to her.

Because if she had children, she'd have to give them a home. And ideally, though not necessarily, she needed a partner to have them with. And she certainly couldn't carry a child around with her as well as her backpack. So with so many obstacles to overcome, it really wasn't something she'd given much thought to.

Teo didn't press for a longer answer for which she was grateful. He put the champagne glasses and bottle down on a low table near an armchair and walked back to the threshold, where he slid his arms around her and pulled her tightly to him.

Teo pressed both his lips to her lower one and tugged gently. She opened her mouth yet Teo still kissed everywhere but her lips; her earlobes, her neck, her temples, until finally he brought his mouth back to her hungry lips.

They moved into his room and Cara pulled him to the bed, desperate to feel him on top of her. But he kept them standing, as he kissed and caressed his way up her arms and down her shoulders, over her body, removing her clothing as he went.

It felt as though her insides were unravelling. It was like this with Teo, slow, teasing, she was impatient but he seemed to have all the time and willpower in the world. It made her desperate and satisfied at the same time.

Finally, he pulled her to the bed and onto him. Teo's confidence was a turn-on, but his vulnerability made her heart ache. She'd never known anyone like him, someone who could embody so many contrasting traits all at once. Strength, openness, calmness and passion. He took her breath away, when he was tracing soft circles on her breasts as he was doing now, and even when he was standing on the opposite side of the room, fully dressed. A single, easy smile on his beautiful face could suck every breath of air from her.

As he did now. And more. The air smelt like him, the whole space felt like him. And she wanted to stay there with him forever.

Neither of them set an alarm and they both slept late, satiated and relaxed to their bones after the night before.

'You're on holiday. You don't work for me anymore. What will you do?'

'Some preliminary work for Brussels.' The Brussels job was expected to go on for two weeks but she had to sort out her arrangements after that. She'd been offered a job in California and another in Singapore. The Californian one was straightforward but she'd never been to Singapore and she loved the idea of going. Given the languages she knew, most of her work tended to be in Europe and the USA. She'd love to see more of Asia.

The email had come two days ago—a lucrative high-stakes deal with six different parties. Three languages. She should have jumped at it.

So, take the challenge. Go for it!

'What's up?' Teo asked her.

'Why do you ask?'

'You're biting your lip as though I don't feed you enough.'

Cara licked her lips, realising what she'd done. 'Nothing,' she said.

Teo raised an eyebrow. She wanted to talk to him about her dilemma but that would mean talking about *after.*

After she left.

They would both have lives after she left, Teo with his movie and Seville.

Cara with…maybe Singapore.

A year ago, she would've hit Reply to the email accepting the Singapore job with a 'Hell yeah,' but now? Now her fingers didn't seem to be able to type at all.

Because Brussels was close. It was in the same time zone. But Singapore was a hemisphere away and the thought of that made her chest tight.

She didn't want to go. Not next week.

Not ever.

You can't stay. Apart from anything else, Teo doesn't want you to. This is a temporary thing for him. Teo is even less capable of trusting someone than you are.

He has to read every contract fifty times, he's so convinced someone is out to trick him. He won't do anything unless he's checked the contract half a dozen times.

She knew why he was the way he was. His

father's betrayal had caused a wound that may never heal, but understanding why Teo was the way he was didn't mean he was any more likely to change.

It was a shame because if he was willing to trust her then maybe, just maybe, she might be willing to trust him.

The idea of trusting someone made her heart rate spike, but this was Teo. Loyal, proper, steadfast Teo. Teo, who Pablo had respected more than anyone in the world. Teo, who she in turn trusted more than anyone alive.

Teo, who made her laugh, Teo, who had sparked a desire in her she couldn't remember experiencing before in her life.

Teo, who she longed for so much even when he was in the same room as her.

Could she love him? Was this what love felt like? Or was this just what regret felt like? Or was she just anxious because of Pablo, of seeing his parents? Of leaving Seville for the second time? Whatever this emotion was, it had her jittery. Her hands shaking. She pushed her coffee mug away.

'Cara?'

Teo's voice brought her back to earth and snapped her out of her thoughts with a jolt.

'What?'

'You were a million miles away.'

She nodded. Yes, she was. Imagining herself

in Singapore. Far away from Teo. She clicked her laptop shut.

'Sorry, what did you say?'

'I asked if you're okay?' A frown creased his gorgeous brow.

No, she couldn't tell him. That wasn't their arrangement. Besides, she didn't even know where she'd start. She was tired, that was all. She was hardly in a good space to be thinking straight, let alone making any decisions.

'I'm fine, just tired. Someone kept me up half the night.'

He smiled. 'I'm very sorry, though I don't remember hearing any complaints.'

No. Her exact words had been *More. Don't stop.* And *Don't you dare stop.* Her muscles clenched at the memory.

This wouldn't do. None of this would do. She pushed her chair back.

'I just need a walk, some air before the day gets too hot.'

He stood as well.

'Cara?'

'Yes?'

'You can talk to me, you know.'

'About what?'

'About whatever has made you jumpy.'

She smiled and nodded, but she didn't agree at all. Teo was the last person she could talk to about the fears and emotions suddenly rippling through her. Because even though she didn't want to leave, he'd still be able to let her go.

The fan was no match for the heavy afternoon air. They lay as they had fallen after making love, with their heads at opposite ends of the bed, top to tail. It suited him to be close to her, but not too close. He didn't want to have to look into her eyes, afraid of what his might reveal. But at the same time, he wanted her within hand's reach, touching distance. He was afraid of what lay ahead, but at the same time, terrified of her leaving.

Three days.

Three more days.

So all he could focus on were her two pretty feet and her toes wiggling as she chatted to him.

I wonder if she knows that her feet are as expressive as her hands?

Her nails were painted a bright pink, and one even had a tiny picture of a flower painted on it. Her feet were a contrast to her hands, which were on public view and neat, unadorned. Professional.

It's my job to blend in. I'm not meant to stand out.

An impossible task for someone as beautiful as Cara.

And then there was her tattoo. He traced it with his index finger. The sea turtle.

'You like turtles?'

'You don't?'

'I like turtles just fine. But I don't think I'd like one as a pet.'

'Of course not, they belong in the wild.'

'And I don't know that I love them enough to get a tattoo of one.'

'Ah, yes, well that, my friend, is how we're different.'

Friend? Two weeks ago, the word would have made him smile, now it crushed him.

'Turtles have their home on their back. They are self-contained. They have everything they need.'

'Like you,' he whispered.

'Yep. And of course it's cute.'

Cara would never stay in Seville, even if he begged. She'd never lose her shell. Or her backpack. She couldn't. She was that turtle.

The next morning, they lingered at the kitchen table, breakfast long eaten. She was reading something on her laptop; he was making an unhurried start on his emails.

He'd miss this. His days were so much nicer when she was near. Even as they were now, in silence but working alongside each other. Everything was better.

'Oh.' Cara gasped.

'What's happened?'

She stared at her screen and he watched her face turn from shock to grief.

He felt her pain in his gut, even though he didn't even know what was wrong.

'It's an email from my lawyer.'

Anger began simmering up inside Teo but he kept his expression as neutral as possible.

'What's happened?'

'They've heard from Liam. Oh, Teo.' Cara slumped over her laptop, face in her hands. Teo stood and wrapped his arms around her. She pushed her laptop towards him with the offending email open.

Teo scanned it. The lawyers appeared professional and sympathetic but the news wasn't good.

Her half-brother had sold the family home. That, in itself wasn't great but the next line was heartbreaking. It had been sold to a developer who had already demolished it to build six condominiums.

'I wasn't expecting great news, I wasn't expecting him to give in, but I wasn't expecting this,' she said.

'I'm so sorry. I'll get my own lawyers to look at it. We'll fight for a share of the proceeds.'

She pushed him away.

'It's not about the money. It's about the house. It's the only home I've ever had. And he sold it! Without even telling me!'

'I'm so sorry.' He was gutted for a house he'd never seen.

'We can fix this.'

She smiled but shook her head. 'We can't, Teo. Not with all the money or will in the world.'

'Then we'll...'

'What? You know there's nothing to be done.'

She'd lost more than a house; she'd lost the only home she would ever have and nothing he could ever do would replace that.

You could give her a home. Here.

He was still reeling from his own thought when Cara pushed back her chair and stood.

'I think I need a walk.'

'Do you want me to come?'

She shook her head.

He hated to watch her go, hated seeing her pain.

He could give her a home. He wanted to, but she was a turtle. She'd never stay in one place now.

'You don't have to do this alone. I'm here. For anything you need. I can fight for you or sit with you. Anything.'

Cara turned back to him, rested her hand on his arm and squeezed.

'I know,' she said, but she turned and left anyway.

Teo dropped back into his chair. He could help her. Couldn't she see? She could trust him!

Trust you to what? To look after her. Feed her? He couldn't even fix this. Her house. Her brother. Besides, why would Cara trust him? He was a doer. An organiser. He wasn't brilliant.

Like Pablo.

'Oh, I thought you'd both left,' said Alba. His housekeeper began cleaning up the breakfast dishes.

'Cara's gone for a walk. I'm on my way out.' He stood again.

'She didn't look happy.'

Typical Alba way of digging for information.

'She's just had some bad news. She just found out her childhood home has been demolished.'

Alba nodded but didn't seem too concerned. 'Houses come and go.'

He laughed. 'Sure, but this one we're standing in is at least a hundred and fifty years old.'

'Sure, but it's been home to many people before you. Home isn't a building, it's what's in your heart.'

He knew this, but it would be a totally insensitive thing to say to Cara at this moment in time. Cara's house was more than a home, a safe refuge, it was her parents, it was her childhood. It was all her formative memories. And to lose it because of a betrayal by her closest relative was really heartbreaking.

And he couldn't fix it.

She doesn't need you to. She's independent.

'This would make a nice home for her,' Alba said.

Teo laughed. 'Wow, you're not holding back.'

She shrugged. 'Why would I do that? She

leaves the day after tomorrow, so you'd better get your act together.'

'I don't need to get anything together. She's going to leave. She has another job to get to.'

This isn't the home she wants. She wants the one that's currently a building site for several condos.

Besides, why would she trust you? You're betraying your oldest friend by being with her and your father was a criminal.

'You worry way too much about what other people think. The only thing that matters is what you think,' Alba said.

It reminded him of Val's words: *the most important thing is how she feels.*

His feelings, her feelings, they were two independent souls. It would be impossible to make it work.

She was a turtle, and he built castles with other people's dreams.

Cara took the same route she and Teo had been accustomed to in the evenings. It was different in the morning, cooler, quieter. The street-sweepers were still at work on the streets, many of the shutters still closed. Her feet knew the way though. The same circuit to the local park and back. She'd only been here a few weeks and yet she had a routine.

Having a routine, being comfortable in a place,

usually made her restless. It meant she was in danger to settling down. Of stopping. Of slowing. But now, there was nowhere to go back to. No home. No Woods Hole. No parents. She picked up her pace and walked faster. She'd choose a different route today. She wasn't going to settle anywhere. She turned a different corner.

Cara strode on. Her body felt strong, fully recovered now from the appendicitis, and the surgery a distant memory. She admired the unfamiliar streets, the new, different square with its unfamiliar church. And on she went, down another old alleyway, past a new park. This was good. This was how she lived, a new vista around each corner. Always something else to discover. It was good, she was fine. And she didn't need her house.

Cara's mouth was parched, she realised too late she should have taken a hat with her, the sun was getting higher and the air warmer. It was time to head home.

She turned and began to retrace her steps.

Except…the streets were not familiar. She reached for her phone to find her route home but her heart rate increased as she felt over her body and couldn't locate it. She felt herself again but it still wasn't there. She hadn't taken her bag and had left Teo's house without anything at all.

She didn't have her phone with her. She didn't have a map.

She had nothing. And was tired and thirsty and felt like a good cry. She walked around another corner and a large church came into view. She recognised the Basílica de la Macarena, a place she'd visited a decade ago and realised how far away from home she was.

After weighing up all her options she walked into a souvenir shop, told the woman she was lost and asked if she could please use her phone for a call. Seconds later she was speaking to Teo.

'Hi, it's me. Cara.'

'What's wrong? Where are you?'

'Lost.'

'Where? I'll come and get you.'

'I'm sorry, I left my phone at home.'

'Don't apologise. Where are you?'

'The Basílica de la Macarena.'

'I'll be right there.'

She handed the phone back to the woman.

Teo did arrive quickly, or so it seemed. Cara hadn't even had time to think of an explanation for getting lost, but as soon as he arrived, she realised she didn't need one. He jumped straight out of his car and went to her, enfolding her in a tight hug.

'I'm sorry,' she said into his chest.

He stroked her head. 'Please stop saying that.'

'I forgot my phone.'

'I understand, you just had some awful news.'

His understanding and lack of blame made her

press herself closer to him. She hadn't realised how worried she'd been to have been lost until he was there, holding her. His familiar body a sanctuary.

'You can call me anytime, anywhere, I will come.'

She didn't doubt that he meant those words, yet once she pulled away and they got into the car, she felt foolish all over again.

She would never call him for help again. She mustn't. Because even though her feelings for Teo were becoming increasingly strong and heavy to bear, Teo didn't feel the same way. As best she was a short-term fling, at worst a responsibility he owed to his oldest friend. Either way, it wouldn't be fair on either of them.

Cara sat on the edge of her bed, wrapped in her robe, hair still damp. She should start getting ready. She should be excited about going to a ball, but she didn't seem to be able to muster the energy or the motivation to dry her hair or put on her make-up.

This deep sense of exhaustion had been with her since yesterday and the news from her lawyers. It didn't help that this was her last night in Spain. It felt as though the last month had finally caught up with her, the surgery, Teo…and now Liam.

You'll feel better tomorrow, once you're on the road again. You'll feel like yourself.

That was all it was. This time with Teo had been great, but it hadn't been real life. She'd been unwell, and that had wreaked havoc with her emotions. No wonder she was feeling drained. And confused. It wasn't because she was developing feelings for Teo. It couldn't be. He was cold and distant Mateo Ortiz. Pablo's grumpy friend.

And yet, she was thinking about him. All the time. Even in her dreams.

Get some distance from him and you'll forget him soon enough.

Because she had to. Because whatever she might or might not feel for Teo, he was not remotely in the same place as her and probably never would be. The fact that he didn't want her to come to the ball proved this and was probably why she was still sitting on her bed in her robe.

There was a knock at the door and her heart hitched. She could tell him that she'd changed her mind, that it was better if she didn't go. He was right. It would be awkward for both of them and why put themselves through it when they both knew that tomorrow she'd be getting on a plane. He didn't want her there, not really.

But it wasn't Teo. It was Alba. 'I've come to see if you need any help getting into your dress, but look at you, you're not even close to being ready.'

'I'm not feeling the best.'

'Nonsense. This is just big night nerves. Everyone gets them.'

Not like this.

Alba started fussing around, clearing room on Cara's dresser and pulling up a chair. 'Let's get you sorted. Come on, you sit here and do your make up while I do your hair.'

Cara did as she was told and sat down in front of the large mirror.

Out of nowhere, Alba produced a blow-dryer and a brush and went to work, sectioning, drying, curling.

'Are you going to wear it up or down?' Alba asked.

'I wasn't really sure.'

'Then let's see how it looks down, if not, we can do it up. You'd better get going with your make-up.'

Cara was shamed into picking up her bag and sorting through it for a moisturiser and a primer.

'Not that you need much. Love, you never do, but I expect you want to feel special tonight.'

Cara did want to feel special tonight, but no amount of make-up was going to fix the heavy ball in her stomach.

'It's just another night,' she mumbled.

'Then why are you so anxious?'

Had she told Alba she was nervous? Or had her behaviour just hinted at it?

She wasn't nervous about the ball as such, more

about the knowledge that this was her last night in Seville. Her last chance to say something to Teo. But what on earth would she say?

I think I might be in love with you. Does that scare you?

She knew his answer even before she asked the question. Oh, he cared for her. Just not enough.

'I'm more sad than nervous. I'm leaving tomorrow.'

Alba said nothing over the roar of the hairdryer. She worked Cara's hair while Cara paid special attention to her make-up. After Cara finished and finally focused away from matters of eyeliner and contours, she looked at Alba's work. Her golden hair fell down in luxurious shiny waves. She gasped.

'I can never get it to look like that. How did you do it?'

Alba shrugged 'I have three daughters and six granddaughters. I've had some practice. Now should we get you into that dress?'

The gold dress was hanging from the top of the wardrobe. It was gorgeous, but what had she been thinking buying it? And all the other things she'd bought while she had been here. She couldn't take any of it with her. None of her new things would fit in her backpack. Besides, what use would a red flamenco dress be at business meetings in Brussels or Singapore?

Alba brought the dress over to her and helped

Cara step into it. Alba adjusted the neckline, instructed Cara to hold her bust in place and then zipped it up at the back. She stepped away and let Cara look at herself in the mirror. Alba clutched her hands to her chest. 'Beautiful.'

Did she look beautiful enough to make Teo fall in love with her?

Nothing you can say or do will make him do that. You could be the most beautiful woman in the world in the most beautiful dress and he still wouldn't love you.

Her eyes began to fill but she swallowed the tears back down. Alba interpreted her reaction as regret, instead of heartbreak.

Teo's kindness and care over the last day since she found out about the house had been amazing and only made her pain worse. Dropping everything to come and pick her up when she'd gotten herself lost. Holding her, just being with her.

'You don't have to leave, you know.'

'I do. My time here is over. I'm well again, I have another job to get to.'

'So?'

'So I have to leave.'

Alba shrugged again.

Maybe you don't have to, her shrug suggested. Maybe, just maybe, if she told Teo what was on her mind she could stay?

'I don't want to stay,' Cara said, answering a comment Alba hadn't even made.

'Fair enough. Who would want to stay here, in this beautiful house? With a wonderful man.'

Cara shook her head. No. It was time to move on. It wasn't unusual to feel regret about leaving a place but that regret always dissipated when she arrived somewhere new and found a whole new set of things to explore.

Just like she would tomorrow evening when she arrived in Brussels. Teo would start to become a memory. Just like her parents and Pablo and her house. Something that existed in the past only.

Only right now she couldn't imagine ever forgetting him at all.

CHAPTER ELEVEN

CARA EXPECTED THE ball to be held inside in a generic conference space, the likes of which she'd seen all over the world, but this was not that at all. The ball was being held in the large courtyard of a grand hotel, surrounded by arches, decorated in mosaics and carved in fine Moorish detail. They stood under the sky and a canopy of fairy lights, strung across the courtyard. The music was loud enough to dance to, but not to interrupt the conversation. The whole place smelt of Seville and its famous perfume of orange blossom and jasmine. It was magical.

The weight in Cara's stomach grew a little heavier. She should just enjoy the evening, live in the moment, but her future began tomorrow and it was difficult to look past that.

A voice called from behind. 'Teo, darling!'

Teo dropped her hand like it was on fire, stood ramrod-straight and they both turned in the direction of the voice. It was a middle-aged couple, a head shorter than her and Teo. Well-groomed, looking expectant.

Pablo's parents.

Pablo's mother and Cara recognised one another in the same blink. Señor Pascal's memory was not as clear as his wife's because he said, 'Teo, my boy. It's so lovely to see you. And who is your date?'

Teo recoiled subtly, and Cara cleared her throat. 'Señor Pascal, it's Cara McCartney. I'm not sure if you remember me. I used to be friends with your son.'

Señor Pascal's mouth dropped but his wife leant in to kiss Cara on both cheeks.

'Cara, darling, of course we remember you. We're simply surprised to see you.'

'I'm sorry I didn't let you know I was here. It's been…well, my visit hasn't exactly gone to plan.'

Señora Pascal touched Cara's arm. 'It's a lovely surprise, don't get me wrong.'

Cara explained the circumstances of her visit, how she had come to be staying with Teo, her agreement to work for him. 'I'm very glad I had the chance to see you both tonight.'

Cara was aware of Teo's posture becoming increasingly stiffer next to her. She hardly dared look at him and certainly couldn't show any affection. It was as though a glass wall had risen up between them. Bulletproof. Impenetrable.

'Could you all excuse me? I have to greet a

few people and I'm sure you have a lot to catch up on,' he said.

And he was gone. Leaving her alone with Pablo's parents.

'It's been too long,' Señor Pascal said.

Since the funeral, Cara thought, but didn't say it out loud.

'How have you both been?' She regretted the question as soon as it was out of her mouth. They had lost their only son, that wasn't something anyone moved on from lightly.

Señor Pascal slipped silently away and Cara wanted to disappear into the checkerboard tiles beneath her feet. Cara's loss had been deep as well, but she'd been young. Her relationship with Pablo had been intense, but short.

Señora Pascal squeezed Cara's arm. 'Oh, you know. We still have our bad days. We never forget him, but we've learned to live with his loss. And evenings like tonight, they are hard, but also very wonderful.'

Cara nodded. She knew exactly what Pablo's mother meant. 'Yes. What Val and Teo have done in Pablo's memory is amazing, but it must bring everything up as well.'

'Yes.' She sniffed back some tears. 'Oh, don't mind me, I just didn't expect to see you tonight. And you must think me so rude, what have *you* been doing with your life?'

Señor Pascal reappeared at their side. Far from

being upset, he brought over three champagne flutes and handed them to Cara and his wife with a smile.

'Cara, it's truly wonderful to see you.'

She caught them up on her life for the past decade, on her work and her travels.

'You were always welcome to come and visit,' Señor Pascal said.

'But we understand that the accident was traumatic for you too. We were—are—always there for you as well. Even though Pablo is gone,' added Pablo's mother.

Cara felt pressure build behind her eyes, in her nose. She sniffed it away as well but Señora Pascal pressed one of her tissues into Cara's hand.

'Thank you. That means a lot.'

That was an understatement. Why hadn't she gone back to see these wonderful, generous people?

Because they were more of a family to you than your own and it hurt too much to rely on them. They aren't your family and never can be.

When she'd left Seville the day after Pablo's funeral, she'd flown straight back to the States and her next semester of college. She'd been fleeing from something then. This time she had the opportunity to say goodbye to everyone and the city of Seville properly.

'I'm leaving again tomorrow, but I promise

I won't leave it so long again between visits,' she said.

'Tomorrow?' Pablo's mother asked. 'But when will you be back?'

'I don't know.'

The Pascals exchanged a look.

'I envy you, Cara. The freedom to go where you want to go, to do what you want.'

She smiled. Yes. She had all the freedom in the world, didn't she?

Then why did she feel so sad? Freedom was wonderful, yet it could also be lonely.

'You can do anything you want to do,' Pablo's mother said.

And in that moment, Cara realised she was right. She could do anything. Besides, what did she really have to lose when she'd already lost everything? Her parents, her home.

If you're going to leave anyway, shouldn't you just tell him how you feel?

The Pascals were telling Cara all about the work of the foundation but she couldn't concentrate. She'd decided. After days of confusion and sadness, she suddenly knew what she needed to do.

Teo mingled with the guests, caught up with people he hadn't seen since the year before, but his body remained on the watch for Cara. She spoke with the Pascals for a while but then she was on her own.

You're her date, you have to go to her. It's rude to abandon her like that in a crowd of people she doesn't know.

He wanted nothing more than to be at her side, except…when he was next to her, he felt all the eyes on him, the camera flashes pointed in their direction. Everyone naturally wanted to know who the beautiful woman he'd brought with him was. Of course they did. She lit up the room.

'Who is your beautiful friend?' asked a woman who headed up one of their literacy programs.

'Her name is Cara McCartney. She's an interpreter, working with Val and I for a while.'

The woman smiled. 'She was talking to Pablo's parents earlier. Does she know them?'

Did nothing escape these people?

'Yes, she is an old friend of Pablo's.'

'Ah, I see.'

Yes, Cara would always be Pablo's ex. Pablo would always be the reason for their connection.

'You should go to her, instead of talking to an old lady like me.'

'Nonsense. It's lovely to see you,' he said.

'You don't have to be working all the time, Teo. You are allowed to enjoy yourself.'

The woman slipped away, no doubt to spread the news that the beautiful woman in the gold dress whom Teo had brought to the ball had a connection to Pablo.

He'd seen the look on Emilio Pascal's face when he'd noticed him holding hands with Cara. He'd seen the way Anita Pascal had looked at them both. Shocked. Surprised.

None of that was meant to happen. He hadn't meant to flaunt his relationship with their dead son's girlfriend in their faces. Especially not at the Pablo Pascal Foundation Annual Ball.

But none of these thoughts stopped him from winding his way through the crowd to where Cara stood, alone.

'Are you okay?' Teo leant in to whisper to her but was careful not to touch her.

'Yes, I mean, it was emotional talking to them, but I'm okay.' Her eyes were tinged with red and she was clutching a wet tissue. He *knew* bringing her here was a bad idea.

'I'm sorry you had to see them. If you need to leave, I understand.'

'Why would I leave?'

'Because the Pascals are here, seeing them has upset you.'

She took a deep breath. 'I've told you, I'm not going to break. It was good to see them, really.'

But she was upset. And he hated that it was his fault.

'You don't have to put yourself through this.'

She looked at him directly, held his attention

with a glare. 'I'm not putting myself through anything, I want to be here. I can handle this. It's emotional, but it's also really, really good to see them after all these years.'

Teo frowned. 'Do they know about us?' he asked.

He knew instantly from her expression that it was the wrong thing to ask.

'I didn't tell them anything but I have no idea. And so what if they do?'

'Cara, I hardly think you and I flaunting our relationship in front of Pablo's parents is a good idea.'

'We haven't flaunted anything!' she hissed. 'I haven't told anyone anything about us and we haven't so much as brushed against one another since we arrived. Do you want me to stay?' She looked hurt, but this could be the out they both needed. If she was upset maybe she should leave.

'I want you to do what's best for you.'

'I know that, Teo. I know you are selfless to the point of stupidity. But I'm asking you what you want. Forget for a moment what you think I want or what you think the right thing is, what do you want?'

The most important thing is, what do you want?

'I want what's best for you.'

'Gah, Teo. No. This is never going to work if you can't be honest. If not with me, at least with yourself.'

Teo drew a breath to argue, to tell her that he was so honest with himself about his shortcomings, about his failures, about everything, that if she knew some of the things he told himself she'd think he was too honest.

But he didn't because they were in a crowd of people and also because at that moment Val appeared at their side and greeted Cara with a kiss.

'Great night, well done,' he said to Teo.

'Well done you,' Teo replied.

Val snorted. 'I did nothing, we all know that when it comes to organising things like this—or organising anything in fact—that you are the organiser.'

He was just the organiser. Great. Now he felt even smaller than he had moments before. Val and Pablo were the geniuses, he was just the organiser.

A woman, a stranger, appeared at Cara's side and asked about her dress. Cara's attention turned and the women began talking.

'You're setting tongues wagging.'

'What do you mean?'

'Everyone wants to know who the beautiful woman in gold is.'

'And what have you told them?'

Val pulled a face. 'The truth.'

'Which is what exactly?'

Teo's hands tingled as his adrenaline levels spiked.

'That she used to date Pablo—'

'You lead with that?'

'Why not? This is the Pablo Pascal Foundation Ball in case you hadn't noticed. What should I have said?'

'That she's been working with us, perhaps?'

'Or that you're head over heels in love with her?' Val whispered.

'What?'

'I didn't say that. I wanted to. But I didn't.'

'Good, because it isn't true.'

Val laughed. 'Sure, besides, I think everyone can make their own mind up.'

'What do you mean?'

'You may as well have a neon sign above your head. Everyone's noticed it.'

Teo's jaw was tight. His hands clenched. He wanted to get out of there before he exploded. Val was way out of line…

'Is she still leaving tomorrow?'

'Why wouldn't she?'

'Because you might have asked her to stay.'

Teo scoffed. 'She can't stay. She has a job in Brussels.'

'But after that?'

'After, she goes to her next job, and the next. She doesn't live anywhere.'

'So, that's perfect. She could live here.'

She could, he was right, base herself in Seville,

and travel from Seville to anywhere she needed to go in the world.

But that would mean he'd miss her when she left. And it would mean his life would become further linked to hers. And people would talk, like they were doing now, about how he was sleeping with his dead friend's ex. About how he had profited from Pablo's creations and now was stealing his girlfriend. About how Teo Ortiz was not the upstanding proper person he tried to make everyone believe. How he really was a thief. How he really was no better than his own father.

Cara made small talk with some other guests, Teo spoke to Val and them some others, but they stayed where they were, in their small circle in the courtyard. Even with their backs turned, she still knew where he was. Her body felt it. Attached by invisible strings that were impervious to all the people coming and going around them.

Her anger from earlier had left her, it had only simmered. Teo wasn't ashamed of her, he was only worried about what other people thought. He was worried about upsetting the Pascals.

But Cara wasn't. Not now she'd seen them.

Yes, they probably did suspect that she and Teo had become close and not only were they not upset, they were delighted.

But it was no use trying to tell Teo that. He had to realise this himself.

If she could make the leap to trusting Teo, then couldn't he? If she could take a chance, surely Teo could as well?

She had to tell him. She was running out of time.

Cara excused herself from the woman she was talking to. She wasn't going to wait another moment. She had to do it now, before she lost her nerve. Teo was with Val and a few other people, so it was easy to go up to him, take his arm and excuse them both from the circle.

Teo didn't protest, she knew he wouldn't, that would only create more interest in them and that was the last thing he wanted to do. She led him to a quiet corner of the courtyard, beside large potted orange trees.

'Are you alright?' he asked.

She bit back a smile. 'I'm fine. I'm good in fact. Great.' No, that was overstating things. Whether she was great would depend on his reaction to what she was going to say next.

'Teo, I love you. I'm in love with you. And I thought you should know, before I leave.'

Teo's jaw dropped, shock crossed his face but in a second, he restored his neutral expression.

She'd been so sure that telling him was the right thing to do, she hadn't thought of what would happen next.

Of this moment.

She hadn't expected him to say, 'Thank you for telling me.'

'Thank you?' Was he serious?

Yes, this is Teo, he's always serious.

'Do you love me?' she prompted. She had nothing to lose.

'Cara, I…'

'It's a yes or no question, Teo.'

'It's more complicated than that.'

'How? Yes or no. Do you have feelings for me?'

'Of course I do. You know I do.'

'And do you love me?' Why couldn't he just admit it? If he loved her, they could figure things out, they could come up with a plan for the future, something that worked for both of them. If he loved her, they could do this together, but as long as he held back on her, they couldn't.

Teo grimaced and her heart fell.

'Because, Teo, I love you. I love you deeply and surprisingly. I love you so much and I don't want to live without you. But I can't do this alone. I need to know if you feel the same way. Or if you think one day you might feel the same way.'

'Cara, can we talk about this later?' he said and her knees buckled.

'There is no later. I'm getting on a plane tomorrow.'

'Just not here.'

Of course not, not when other people were around.

'I'm telling you I'm prepared to be wherever in the world you are. I'm prepared to upend my life. And you…'

Even if he couldn't name it, what they had was love. There was no other word—not in any language—to describe it.

'Cara, you know it's far more complicated than just saying three words.' He spoke softly.

But it wasn't. It really was just that simple.

'Here you both are!' Jerry's booming voice made them both turn. 'Teo, Val's looking for you. They need to start the speeches. And I promised this beautiful woman a dance.'

The last thing Cara felt like was dancing, but at least she didn't have to stay and listen to Teo tell her that he didn't love her. And that she had been right all along, she would always be alone.

Teo watched as Jerry led Cara away to the dance floor. His heart was still in his throat. She loved him? The thought should have made him fly, except just thinking about his response to her made him want to crawl into the nearest hole.

Unfortunately, standing on a floor of UNESCO-protected tiles made this impossible. Particularly as in a few minutes he was expected to stand up in front of two thousand people and talk about Pablo. Especially since Pablo's parents were walking towards him now.

'It's so lovely to see you with Cara,' Anita Pascal said.

He opened his mouth to deny it. But lying was even more difficult than telling the truth.

'You're not upset?' he asked.

'Why would we be?' Emilio shook his head.

'Because of Pablo.'

'That's exactly why we're pleased. We know he would be too.'

'Would he?'

'Son, you know better than anyone what a remarkable person Pablo was. He was many things, but he certainly wasn't petty or jealous. He would want you to be happy, and Cara as well.

'I've taken everything from him. I owe him everything.'

'You owe him nothing. You didn't take anything from him, you grew his ideas, developed them, built them into a wonderful thing.'

'Two wonderful things,' Anita added. 'The company and the foundation. You didn't steal his idea. You grew it. With Val. Pablo wanted this business, he'd be so grateful that you made it what it is.'

'Look around you,' Emilio said. 'Everyone here knows you loved Pablo. Teo, you have nothing left to prove. We all know the business and the foundation wouldn't exist without you. You may have built it with your friends' skills and creations, but it wouldn't exist without you. You are as integral to all of this as they are.

'Besides,' continued Emilio, 'no one thinks you've stolen Cara. Heavens, that girl has a mind of her own.'

Teo smiled.

She definitely did. And it was one of the many reasons he loved her.

He loved her. And he had to tell her. Immediately.

Teo sought Cara out on the dance floor but couldn't see her golden dress anywhere. With dismay, he noticed Jerry standing with Doug to the side of the dance floor.

'Where's Cara gone?' Teo asked the men.

Jerry shrugged. 'She said she had to leave.'

'Leave?'

'Yes, she said goodbye, told us how much she'd loved working with us and wished us well.'

Damn.

'It was only a few moments ago, I'm sure she hasn't left yet.'

Teo wasn't. He couldn't blame her for getting out of here as soon as possible, especially after he'd just behaved so badly.

Thank you.

What had he been thinking?

He'd been thinking of his own hesitation, his own issues. When he should have only been thinking of her. He should have pulled her to him and promised to love her forever.

Teo was tall enough to see over many heads, but his height was not a match for the crowd. He had to go higher.

He climbed the first half of a nearby staircase and searched for the gold of her dress and the golden flames of her hair.

There she was. At the other end of the courtyard. Heading to the exit. Instantly realising he'd never be able to weave his way across the heaving dance floor to catch her, he climbed the rest of the marble staircase and ran along the length of the balcony.

There she was below him, just about to disappear underneath it and out of the ball.

'Cara, stop! Don't leave.' *I love you.*

She didn't stop and he now realised there was no staircase back down to the courtyard at this end.

There was no way he'd get down in time to stop her.

You'll catch her at home.

No. That wasn't good enough. Teo went to the balustrade and leant over it. 'Cara! Cara McCartney!' he cried.

Some guests stopped and looked up but Cara didn't.

'Cara! Cara! Someone stop that woman in gold!' he yelled again.

A few people looked around but no one close enough to catch her. The music drowned out his voice.

A metal box caught his eye. The circuit board. Could it be the power? All the power? He flipped it open and scanned the board. He only had an instant and flicked the switch marked 'Power 1.'

There was the clack of electricity turning off and music winding down. The place was quiet but for the voices, which all wondered what was going on.

The only lights that remained on were the fairy lights, strung across the courtyard, presumably on a different circuit but he couldn't think about that now.

'Cara, Cara, please stop.'

But she had already, like everyone else, frozen to the spot where she stood and was looking around to see what was wrong.

'Cara, please don't leave,' he yelled.

Her eyes found his and even from this distance he could tell she wasn't convinced.

'Don't leave. Not now. Not ever.'

She stood still, and he was now aware that everyone else had seen who he was talking to.

'Teo, are you serious?'

'I am serious, deeply serious. I love you and I want you to stay. Forever.'

He was aware of everyone in the ball looking from Cara to him and back again, but all he saw, as the rest of the world and all his concerns and worries fell away, was Cara standing where she was, nodding. And smiling.

Cara's limbs were weak. Every set of eyes in the courtyard were on her but she only had time for one pair. She pushed her way through the crowd to the nearest staircase but it was like wading through mud. Everyone wanted to greet her and give their best wishes but she couldn't get to Teo fast enough.

What on earth had he been thinking? Declaring his love from the balcony? In front of everyone? One minute he was telling her it was impossible, the next this. She should…she should…but the heartache she'd felt five minutes ago was all forgotten. He loved her. He loved her enough to tell the world. He loved her enough not to care what the rest of the world thought.

With a loud snap, the big lights came back on. Cara squinted, momentarily losing her focus on the staircase.

But then there he was, bounding down the last steps in a single leap and heading in her direction.

When they finally reached one another, she fell into his arms and he pulled her tight.

'I'm never letting you go again,' he whispered into her hair. 'I'm so sorry I was such a fool.'

'You were a fool, but I understand it. I understand why. It's been difficult for both of us.

I should've told you earlier how I feel, I should have let you know about my feelings and my fears.'

Teo shook his head. 'I held back too. I held back for so long. I could hardly expect you to tell me how you felt when I was so adamant I wasn't looking for anything serious. I'm so glad you told me. It was the kick I needed, even if it did take me a moment to realise.'

Cara shook her head. 'I wanted to tell you for ages but I couldn't find the words. And tonight's my last night. I panicked. I should have realised that you were already anxious enough about tonight. I could have chosen my moment better.'

He laughed. 'Oh, Cara, you can tell me how you feel anytime and anywhere.'

'Kiss her! Kiss her!' The voice came from across the courtyard but was unmistakenly Val's. A cheer echoed around the four walls of the courtyard.

Teo looked at her and her insides swooped. This was it.

'May I?'

'Oh, Teo, I wish you would.'

A smile broke across his beautiful face like the clouds parting and the sun shining through. She loved his smile, but his smile when it was for her was her new favourite thing in the world. Teo brushed her cheek with the back of his fingers, pushed her tears away with the soft pad of his thumb. She slid her arms around his neck and let herself fall into his gaze. She was aware of one of his strong arms sliding its way around her back, holding her up.

He'll never let you fall.

And when his mouth met hers, she knew he was the last man she'd ever kiss again.

EPILOGUE

It was another perfect spring evening when Alba helped Cara get ready for her wedding in the guest bedroom of the pink house.

Cara had long since moved her life upstairs to the room that was now Teo's and hers. One of the other rooms was now her study where she ran her business, an agency for freelance interpreters, which had become more successful than Cara could have imagined. She still did jobs herself, but picked and chose depending on the client, the job and the location. Teo sometimes went with her, especially for longer jobs. Together they had been to Buenos Aires, Montreal and Singapore.

But each time she returned to the same place, the pink house on the square in Santa Cruz, Seville.

Anita and Emilio Pascal walked Cara from the guest bedroom out into the courtyard where Teo was waiting with his mother, brother and sisters, and a small group of their friends, including Alba and Geraldo.

After celebratory drinks, the party walked the small distance to a restaurant they had hired for the intimate reception, Cara and Teo both adamant that Alba was a guest at this occasion. The speeches were short. Teo thanked everyone for coming, and Cara gave a toast to the people who weren't there in person but who she knew would have been delighted for them, her parents and Pablo.

And later, when they had returned to the pink house, and made love for the first time as a married couple, Cara said, 'I have to show you something.'

Cara rolled over, sat up and lifted her foot to show Teo.

'You got another tattoo,' he said.

Her smile was shy.

'Another turtle. You must really love turtles.'

Why would she get a second house-carrying-creature on her gorgeous skin? Especially now her backpack was stored away in one of the many cupboards of the house.

'It has a mate. A turtle friend.'

Ah, it was starting to make sense.

'My turtle isn't alone anymore. It still carries its house with it, but now it has a forever friend.'

She looked at him, her eyes expectant and he pulled her to him.

He didn't need reminding of her love, Cara was already tattooed over every inch of his body. But he loved the second turtle. He loved being her best friend, one half of a pair. 'I have something for you too.'

They had made a pact of no gifts; guests were invited to donate money to the foundation in lieu of gifts.

'We said no presents!'

'This isn't from me.'

'Then who?'

'I wasn't sure when to give it to you, but here goes.'

Teo rolled over to his bedside table and rolled back holding a velvet box. Long and large. It looked like a jewellery box, yet her wedding and engagement rings were on her finger.

And he said it wasn't from him.

She took the box and lifted the lid.

She gasped. Not quite believing what she was seeing.

Teo looked at her, expectantly. Maybe a little anxious.

Her mother's jewellery.

Her mother's treasures. The last time she had seen these was when she'd foolishly left the box behind at the Woods Hole house before going to college.

A small pair of ruby earrings, several gold chains, and her mother's wedding and engagement rings.

'How?'

'I got in touch with Liam.'

Cara's stomach churned.

'And he…he just gave them to you?'

'I told him that they would make an excellent wedding present for you.'

Cara had sent Liam an email letting him know that she and Teo were engaged, but hadn't extended an invitation to the wedding. She'd let him know where she was living, more for the sake of her niece and nephew, should they ever wish to contact her in the future, but she didn't want Liam at her wedding. And Teo knew all of this.

'And he just let you have them? Oh, Teo, you didn't buy them?'

Somehow the idea of having to pay for her own mother's things made her ill.

'No. But I was firm with him. Gently reminded him that you could still take him to court.'

Cara had no intention of doing so, she didn't want to fight anymore; she'd never forgive Liam but it was better for her and her future if she just moved on.

So to have these. Her mother's jewellery…

Teo picked up a ring, set with a large pearl and Cara's throat closed over.

'That was her engagement ring.'

'Oh, darling.'

Teo went to place it back in the box, but she said, 'No, I want to try it. Pearls need to be worn.'

Together they tried the ring on each of her fingers to see if it would fit. Finally, Teo slid it onto the ring finger on her right hand where it sat perfectly.

'A perfect fit,' Cara said.

'Just like us,' Teo said, and he kissed her.

* * * * *

Look out for the next story in the
Cinderellas in Seville duet

Match Made in Seville *by Michele Renae*

Available now!

And if you enjoyed this story, check out these
other great reads from Justine Lewis

Italian Tycoon to Remember
Dating Game with Her Enemy
How to Win Back a Royal

All available now!